"Your Skin Is Warm, Emily. And Soft."

So were her insides, she thought.

His thumb traced the line of her jaw. "Shall we?" he murmured.

Her heart skipped a beat, than began to race. Wasn't this why she'd come here? To be close to Dylan, to gain his confidence by whatever means necessary?

Shall we?

His voice, his touch, seduced her. Made her want when she had no right to want. Made her tremble with need when she needed desperately to keep her composure.

"Here?"

He lifted his head, stared at her with a mixture of amusement and desire. "Well, normally we begin the palace tours in the reception hall and ballroom, but if you'd like to start here…"

Dear Reader,

'Tis the season to read six passionate, powerful and provocative love stories from Silhouette Desire!

Savor *A Cowboy & a Gentleman* (#1477), December's MAN OF THE MONTH, by beloved author Ann Major. A lonesome cowboy rekindles an old flame in this final title of our MAN OF THE MONTH promotion. MAN OF THE MONTH has had a memorable fourteen-year run and now it's time to make room for other exciting innovations, such as DYNASTIES: THE BARONES, a Boston-based Romeo-and-Juliet continuity with a happy ending, which launches next month, and—starting in June 2003—Desire's three-book sequel to Silhouette's out-of-series continuity THE LONE STAR COUNTRY CLUB. Desire's popular TEXAS CATTLEMAN'S CLUB continuity also returns in 2003, beginning in November.

This month DYNASTIES: THE CONNELLYS concludes with *Cherokee Marriage Dare* (#1478) by Sheri WhiteFeather, a riveting tale featuring a former Green Beret who rescues the youngest Connelly daughter from kidnappers. Award-winning, bestselling romance novelist Rochelle Alers debuts in Desire with *A Younger Man* (#1479), the compelling story of a widow's sensual renaissance. Barbara McCauley's *Royally Pregnant* (#1480) offers a fabulous finale to Silhouette's cross-line CROWN AND GLORY series, while a feisty rancher corrals the sexy cowboy-next-door in *Her Texas Temptation* (#1481) by Shirley Rogers. And a blizzard forces a lone wolf to deliver his hometown sweetheart's infant in *Baby & the Beast* (#1482) by Laura Wright.

Here's hoping you find all six of these supersensual Silhouette Desire titles in your Christmas stocking.

Enjoy!

Joan Marlow Golan

Joan Marlow Golan
Senior Editor, Silhouette Desire

Please address questions and book requests to:
Silhouette Reader Service
U.S.: 3010 Walden Ave., P.O. Box 1325, Buffalo, NY 14269
Canadian: P.O. Box 609, Fort Erie, Ont. L2A 5X3

Royally Pregnant
BARBARA McCAULEY

Silhouette®
Desire®

Published by Silhouette Books

America's Publisher of Contemporary Romance

Special thanks and acknowledgment are given to Barbara McCauley for her contribution to the CROWN AND GLORY series.

 SILHOUETTE BOOKS

ISBN 0-373-76480-4

ROYALLY PREGNANT

Books by Barbara McCauley

BARBARA McCAULEY,

who has written more than twenty novels for Silhouette Books, lives in Southern California with her own handsome hero husband, Frank, who makes it easy to believe in and write about the magic of romance. Barbara's stories have won and been nominated for numerous awards, including the prestigious RITA® Award from the Romance Writers of America, Best Desire of the Year from *Romantic Times* and Best Short Contemporary from the National Reader's Choice Awards.

To Debbi Rawlins—
Thanks, Deb—this one's for you!

One

"It has to look like an accident."

Emily Bridgewater did not turn around at the man's words. With her back straight and head high, she stood at the edge of the bluff and stared out at the choppy, deep-blue waters, watched the thick, black clouds rise up from the east like a demon's ascent from hell. The scent of wild devil's mint choked the late-afternoon air. Dozens of fishing boats, commercial and pleasure alike, headed for the marina—only a fool would challenge the potential wrath of Mother Nature at sea when the skies turned dark as coal.

Emily shivered, not from the icy breeze that whipped at the hem of her long denim skirt, but from despair. What good could possibly come from deceit? she'd asked herself a hundred times in the past three days. Every time her answer had been the same: none.

And every time she'd seen no other way.

"Did you hear me, Emily?" the man snarled. "You must make certain he believes it was an accident."

Emily turned and faced the man. Sutton was the only name she knew him by, though she doubted it was his real name. She'd guessed him to be at least twenty years older than herself, probably in his early forties. He was tall and lean, wore a tight black T-shirt, black pants, black soldier's boots. He'd shaved his head, and his face was as rough and jagged as the bluffs of Penwyck Island, his expression flat and empty. On his left bicep, he wore a tattoo of a small black dagger.

Who he took his orders from, Emily didn't know, but she was certain that Sutton wasn't in charge. He made no decisions and offered no negotiations. He simply did what he was told, without question.

They expected the same of her.

"I'll do what I can."

He smiled at her defiance, closed the distance between them with three long strides. She nearly flinched when he reached out a hand toward her, then roughly grabbed her chin. With his other hand he touched a loose strand of her thick, dark hair and twirled it around his finger. Emily bit the inside of her mouth, refused to back away.

"You'll do better than that." His gray eyes skimmed her face, then lingered on the top button of her short-sleeved white blouse. "You know what will happen if you don't get us what we want, don't you, sweet Emily? You know what we'll do?''

Emily's heart slammed against her ribs, pounded in her head with the same intensity as the crash of waves on the beach below. ''Yes.''

He pulled a small photograph from his T-shirt pocket and held it in front of her face. ''One more look, so you'll make no mistakes.''

Though she'd already seen the picture of the man this morning, Emily glanced at the snapshot again. Short dark-brown hair, deep-blue eyes, a touch of regal mixed with rugged. The photograph was posed, and he did not smile for the camera. His eyes, those striking eyes, held a great deal of intelligence and just a touch of annoyance.

Dear Lord, how will I ever do this?

Setting her teeth, Emily jerked away from Sutton's touch. ''I won't make a mistake.''

The cell phone strapped to Sutton's belt rang. He turned to answer the call, listened for a moment, then slipped the phone back into its holder. ''It's time.''

She glanced at the paved road beside the stand of trees where they stood, knew that the car would be coming around the steep mountain bend in a few minutes. Her pulse raced.

I can't do this. She felt the panic rise. *I can't.* When she hesitated, Sutton grabbed her by the arm and dragged her toward the rented bike resting against a nearby tree.

''What if something goes wrong?'' she gasped, ignoring the painful grip of the man's large hand.

"You'd better make sure nothing goes wrong," he said tightly. "Now get on the bike."

"But if I'm not hurt, if—"

He swung his fist so quickly, she hadn't time to avoid the blow. His knuckles slammed against her cheekbone, made her head snap back. White-hot stars shot across her vision, and she thought for one horrible moment that she might lose what little food she'd eaten that day. She would have fallen to her knees if he hadn't still been holding her up.

"No more ifs, Emily. *Get on the bike!*"

She brushed away the tears of pain from her eyes, then, with her ears still ringing from Sutton's fist, Emily climbed on the bike he held out for her. She gripped the handlebars, placed her feet on the pedals.

She heard the faint whine of a car's engine, the crunch of tires on pebbles.

Breath held, she waited.

"She's going to be a wicked one, Your Highness. A 'triple ale, double female' night, as my da used ta say." From the back seat of the limousine, Dylan Penwyck glanced up and briefly met Liam McNeil's gaze in the rearview mirror. Liam, born in Ireland but raised on Penwyck Island from the time he was eight, had been driving for Dylan's family more than twenty years. In his early forties, with a leprechaun's smile and a lumberjack's build, Liam was full of Irish wit and aphorisms, not to mention a healthy dose of blarney.

Dylan lifted one dark brow. "Not in front of your mother, I'm sure."

Liam laughed, a dry, cracking laugh that came from too many years of cigarettes and rotgut whiskey. ''Only if he was looking for a frying pan ta blast open the back of his skull.''

Dylan tried to imagine his own mother flattening the back of his father's head with a frying pan, but the image of Queen Marissa wielding a frying pan while she chased King Morgan around the royal pantry simply wouldn't come.

His parents' marriage, though an arranged one, had been happy enough. He'd never once heard his mother raise her voice to his father—or to anyone else, for that matter. One look from the queen inspired a person to move mountains. Though no one would ever dare say the words out loud, Dylan more than suspected who held the true power not only in the marriage, but in the palace household, as well.

But now Dylan's father was ill. King Morgan had finally wakened from the coma he'd slipped into five months ago, but there would be many months, if not years, of rehabilitation and therapy. Since Dylan's Uncle Broderick had assumed control of the palace, there'd been overwhelming chaos. And even though Broderick had been ''relieved'' of his duties on the throne, there was much to do to restore order to the palace.

Dylan had cursed himself a thousand times that he hadn't been here these past months, that he'd made himself so inaccessible that even his own family hadn't been able to reach him.

I'm back now, he thought, narrowing his eyes.

And this time he'd stay.

This morning, he'd passed on his sister Meredith's offer to attend a breakfast honoring the head schoolmistress for Penwyck's public education system, and had enjoyed the morning skeet-shooting with Baron and Lady Chaston on their neighboring estate instead. Their daughter, Blair, home from a break at university, had done her best to entice him to stay for lunch, had even batted her baby-blue eyes and pouted when he'd explained he had an urgent meeting at the palace. A complete lie, of course, but Dylan knew that Blair was determined to marry into royalty, and since his fraternal twin Owen had married Jordan Ashbury, Blair had turned her sights on the other royal son—which happened to be yours truly.

She was pretty enough—beautiful even, he supposed, plus she had all the credentials and background for a royal wife. But the woman was out for herself, and the thought of waking up every morning to the shallow bubblehead made Dylan wince.

Dylan had spent the past two years denying the duties and responsibilities he'd been born into. It would have given his parents fits to learn that he'd joined a special forces group in Borovkia, a covert organization called Graystroke that rescued kidnapped dignitaries and businessmen in central Europe. The work had been dangerous and exciting, and with each assignment had loomed the possibility he might not make it back alive, or worse, be kidnapped himself.

Which was why Dylan had falsified identification papers, grown a beard and never told anyone who he really was, neither the men he'd worked with nor his superiors. If they'd known he was Prince Dylan Penwyck, heir to the throne of Penwyck, they never would have sent him out on any assignments. If anything, they probably would have sent him packing. The ransom for a kidnapped prince would be more than the entire economy of many third-world countries.

Dylan turned his attention to the passing countryside, watched the blur of pine trees as they drove up the steep road toward the palace. Past the bluffs, thick, dark clouds rose up over the ocean. Winter had crept in quietly since he'd returned to Penwyck a few weeks ago. Frost in the early morning and a few typical rainstorms, but agreeable temperatures overall.

Today had been especially pleasant. The air had been crisp, but not cold, the skies clear and blue. But anyone who lived on Penwyck Island for more than one winter knew how fickle the weather could be here. Though he'd been gone for the past two years, he'd lived on this island his entire life.

He'd needed to leave Penwyck Island to find out he belonged here. He would never be king, Dylan knew, but he would serve his country and his family, lay down his life, if necessary, to protect and keep them safe.

"The boys and me got a game of five-card draw tonight," Liam said. "You in?"

"I could manage a game or two," Dylan said with a shrug. "Maybe win back some of the pot you snookered me out of the other night."

"With all respect, Your *Royal Highness*," Liam said with a good-natured grin, "me mum's nanny plays a better game than you did. You've no one to blame for your losses but your own self."

Liam was right, Dylan knew. He'd played very poorly. His mind had been everywhere but the game. He'd been concerned about his father's health and his Uncle Broderick's abuse of power once he was on the throne, as well as his brother Owen's kidnapping, his sister's pregnancy and the fact that Owen had a child no one had known about until a few weeks ago.

And that was just for starters. Without a doubt, the palace and the country had been in a major royal upheaval.

"You call me 'Your Royal Highness' like that one more time," Dylan leaned forward in the seat and stared at the winding road ahead, "and I might not let you win even one hand."

"Let *me* win?" Liam choked with laughter as he maneuvered the limo around a sharp turn. "You couldn't—"

"Watch out!"

Later, Dylan might be able to piece together what happened, but at that moment, there was no time to think or to respond. The woman on the bike was suddenly *there*, in the middle of the road. Liam swore as he slammed on the brakes, and even though the car hadn't been going fast, it still swerved. Tires screeched, then skidded those last few feet.

Dylan saw the brunette's startled face, then came the sickening thud as the front of the limo kissed the rear end of the bike. The woman flew in the air, then landed on the other side of the road closest to the bluff.

Dylan was out of the back seat before Liam could jam the car into Park. The woman lay crumpled on her side, her arms and legs limp. Her long, thick, dark hair covered her face like a shroud.

Pulse pounding, Dylan knelt beside her. Dear God, let her be all right, he thought. Gently, he eased the woman to her back, then brushed her hair from her face and placed his hand at the base of her throat.

When he felt the warm, vibrant pulse, Dylan released the breath he'd been holding.

"God have mercy!" An Irish curse on his lips, Liam came running. "Please tell me I haven't killed her."

"You haven't killed her." Dylan kept his voice even and controlled, though his heart was pounding fiercely against his ribs. He quickly swept his gaze over the woman. Her right arm and hand were scraped and bleeding, and an angry red welt bloomed above her left cheekbone. Her blouse was torn and smudged with dirt, her skirt stained with grass.

He glanced back up at her face. Beautiful, was his first impression.

When she moaned and her eyes fluttered open, the word *stunning* grabbed hold of him like a hand around his throat.

Flecks of gray swirled like smoke in her soft-green eyes. Her skin was porcelain-smooth, pale against the mark on her cheekbone. The unseen hand around Dylan's throat tightened further as he looked at her mouth. Lips wide, lush and inviting. A mouth meant for a man's kisses, he thought, then quickly looked back up at her eyes. Confusion swam there, and pain.

"What—" She lifted a hand to her forehead. "What happened?"

"You were crossing the road on your bicycle. Our car struck you." Dylan's stomach twisted as blood trickled down her forehead. He followed the trail of blood to a cut just above her hairline. "Are you in pain?"

"My head," she murmured.

Her eyes slid closed, and for a moment Dylan thought she'd passed out. When she opened them again, relief poured through him.

"Here, take this." Liam pressed a handkerchief into Dylan's hand, then reached into the pocket of his jacket and pulled out a cell phone. "I'll call for an ambulance."

"No." The woman shook her head, then winced from the movement. "There's no need for an ambulance. I just need a minute."

"Be still. Let's at least check for missing limbs, shall we?" Dylan gently dabbed at the blood above her eye, made a stab at levity to help calm the woman. "Hard to ride a bike with only one leg, you know, though I suppose a wooden one works nicely enough. Do you feel this?"

He touched her ankles, noticed that she'd lost one white tennis shoe, though her short sock still hugged her narrow foot.

"Yes." She wiggled her feet. "Your hands are warm."

"I'm going to check if anything's broken," he said, then slid his hands under her long denim skirt. She had the legs of a dancer, he thought, or maybe a runner. Long and curved and well-toned. Her skin was like cool silk. He inched the fabric up to her knees, saw that her right knee was scraped, but there was little blood. "If you like, you can slap me later for being so brazen."

He noted the small ruby-and-diamond ring on her left hand as he slowly raised her arm. When she sucked in a breath at the movement, he gently eased her arm down again.

"I don't suppose I'll be slapping you with that hand," she said through clenched teeth.

When an icy gust of wind from the east struck them, Dylan felt the goosebumps rise on her skin. Fat raindrops splattered on the grass around them, and thunder shook the ground.

"She's going to open up on us any minute." Liam glanced up as a jagged bolt of lightning streaked down and exploded inside a stand of trees less than a quarter mile down the road. They heard the crack of a tree's branch, saw the sparks rise upward on a cloud of smoke. The air, charged with electricity, turned thick and heavy and made the hair on Dylan's arms rise.

"We can't stay here," Dylan yelled over the rising wind and the rumbling of thunder. "I'm going to pick you up and put you in the car."

Another bolt of lightning struck, closer this time, and Liam's prediction proved correct. The sky opened and a torrent of cold rain pounded them. As gently as possible, Dylan scooped the woman up in his arms. She shivered against him, and he held her close, did his best to protect her from the rain as he dashed to the car. Liam held the door open while Dylan laid the woman on the soft, gray leather back seat of the black limo. He climbed in beside her and closed the door.

Bullet-proof glass windows blocked out the raging storm outside. The interior of the car was quiet and warm. Liam jumped into the driver's seat and started the engine.

"Shall I go back for her bike?" Liam asked.

"Later, after the storm subsides." Dylan knelt on the wide floor of the car. "We don't want you to end up like one of those poor moths caught in old Pierre's garden bug zapper."

In just the short run to the car, the woman's dark hair had been drenched and several strands around her pale face had started to curl. When she started to shiver violently, Dylan lifted the lid of a compartment between the seats and pulled out a blanket, then draped it over her shoulders.

"Call ahead for Dr. Waltham," Dylan said over his shoulder. "Tell him what happened and have him waiting by the infirmary entrance."

Liam drove while he made the call. Dylan closed the heavy glass partition between the front seat and the back of the car so the woman wouldn't hear. He saw the pain in her clouded eyes, felt his own frustration knot in his stomach. But there was nothing he could do for her until they got to the palace.

Dammit! He forced himself to concentrate on the woman instead of the car's slow process up the road.

"We'll be there in a few minutes," Dylan said quietly. "Are you comfortable?"

"I'm sorry," she whispered so quietly he barely heard her. "So very sorry."

The intensity in her gaze and the quiet desperation in her voice confused him. He pulled the blanket up and tucked it under her chin. "You have nothing to be sorry for. We hit you, remember?"

She turned away from him. The welt on her face had darkened, and the wound on her head oozed blood.

"What's your name?" He pressed the handkerchief still in his hand to her scalp. "Is there someone we can call?"

Slowly she turned her head back toward him. Dylan saw fear in her gray-green eyes, and confusion, as well.

"I—I don't know."

"You don't know if there's anyone we can call?"

"No." As if in pain, she closed her eyes. "I mean I don't know my name."

Two

What should have been a five-minute ride to the palace had already been fifteen. Dylan silently cursed every bump in the road, every clash of thunder, every kick of wind that sent the limo sliding sideways. Rain fell in heavy sheets, battering the car's roof and windshield. He knew that it was impossible for Liam to safely drive any faster, but that knowledge did little to curb his frustration at the limo's snail's pace up the mountain.

At least the inside of the car was warm and comfortable, Dylan thought as he studied the woman lying on the soft leather seat beside him. He pressed the linen handkerchief to the wound on her head, then frowned at the stark contrast of bright red blood on the white cloth. Lord knew he'd seen more than his share of blood in the past two years—some had even been his own—but this was different. The woman seemed so fragile, so delicate.

And he was responsible.

He'd examined the gash on her head more closely and felt certain that it wasn't too deep. She'd stopped shivering after he'd covered her with the blanket, had even attempted to sit up twice, claiming that she was fine. Both times he'd gently eased her back down onto the seat. She wasn't fine, for God's sake. She'd been hit by a car—*his* car.

Where had she come from? And the bigger question still, who was she?

The fact that she hadn't an answer to that question disturbed him, but she'd taken a nasty fall and blow to the head. It was understandable she was confused and disoriented at the moment.

There was something vaguely familiar about her, though nothing he could put a finger on. Like a tune from his childhood, or an old saying that he hadn't heard in years. It lingered at the edges of his mind, but refused to come closer.

He shook the odd feeling off. Most probably he'd never met her at all. Though it was late in the year, it was possible that she was a tourist, or maybe a guest at one of the neighboring estates. The country-side along the coast of Penwyck was breathtaking. Travellers came from all over the world to view and photograph the scenic cliffs and forests.

But he hadn't noticed a camera, Dylan thought. She hadn't even carried a purse with her.

A blinding bolt of lightning lit the inside of the

car, then thunder crashed. The woman squeezed her eyes shut and huddled beneath the blanket.

"You're all right now," Dylan reassured her, though he wasn't so certain. Her skin had paled and her breathing was shallow. "We'll be at the palace in a few minutes."

"Palace?" Her eyes opened, then narrowed in confusion as she glanced at him.

"Penwyck Palace. That's where my driver and I were headed when you appeared in the road. Do you remember where you were going?"

"I—" She hesitated, then shook her head. "No."

She started to shiver again. Dylan took both her hands in his to comfort as much as warm her cold skin. Her fingers were long and slender, her nails short and neat. Other than the ruby ring on her right hand that he'd noticed before, she wore no jewelry. No wedding ring or evidence that she'd worn one recently, either.

Another bolt of lightning flashed close by. The woman closed her eyes and whimpered.

"Sshh." He squeezed her hands, hoped like hell that she wasn't going into shock.

"Your hands," she said quietly and opened her eyes. "They're so warm."

He smiled at her. "Only because yours are so cold."

A smile flashed at the corners of her mouth, then quickly faded. "You've been so kind, and I don't even know your name."

"Dylan." He checked the wound on her head

again, was relieved that the bleeding had eased.
"Dylan Penwyck."

Her brow furrowed. "Your last name is the same
as the palace you mentioned? Are you a member of
the royal family?"

Even though Dylan had done his best to stay out
of the public eye his entire life, everyone who lived
on this island knew that Dylan Penwyck was King
Morgan Penwyck's son. Not everyone knew exactly
what he looked like, especially since he'd been gone
the past two years, but still, the name *Dylan Penwyck*
was well known to his country's general population.

Unless this woman wasn't from Penwyck, he
thought. Or, possibly, the blow to her head had
wiped out more of her memory than her own name.

But as Liam pulled up in front of the infirmary,
Dylan hadn't time to answer her question, or ask any
more of his own. Wearing a gray rain slicker and
carrying an umbrella, the doctor hurried down the
steps, then quickly opened the car door.

Questions and answers would have to wait for a
while, Dylan knew. He scooped the woman into his
arms and carried her up the infirmary steps while the
doctor shielded her from the rain with his umbrella.
Whatever the beautiful woman's name might be, and
what she'd been doing up on the mountain road,
would have to remain a mystery for a little while
longer.

Thirty minutes later, Dylan stared at the waiting-
room clock and frowned. What the hell was taking
so long? He swore under his breath, then spun on

his heels and continued his pacing. Liam had gone to report the accident to Queen Marissa and Dr. Waltham was still in the examination room.

Dylan's frown deepened, and he stared at the clock again. Surely the doctor had *something* to report by now.

For the hundredth time, Dylan recalled the sound of the car striking the woman's bicycle, the expression of shock on her face just before she flew through the air, then the way her body had crumpled when she'd landed beside the road.

All the cuts and bruises, the blood.

His hands clenched into fists at the memory, then he turned and headed for the examination room at the end of the hall. Enough was enough. He refused to wait any longer. Someone was going to tell him something.

Now.

He lifted his fist to knock on the door, but it opened before he made contact. Mavis Weidermeyer, Dr. Waltham's head nurse, stood on the other side. The woman quite literally filled the doorway.

Damn. Not Mavis, Dylan thought. He'd learned at a young age how to get around most of the staff in the palace, sometimes with charm, sometimes by pulling rank. But nothing worked with Mavis Weidermeyer. There'd been talk that Dr. Waltham's nurse wasn't human, but rather a mechanical military experiment gone awry.

"Your Royal Highness." Nurse Mavis stepped out of the room and closed the door behind her. At six foot, the woman didn't have to look up to meet

Dylan's eye. "Is there something I can help you with?"

If I ever need a piano moved, Dylan thought.

He straightened his shoulders. "I'd like to speak with Dr. Waltham."

"I've already told you that Dr. Waltham will speak to you when he's finished his examination," Mavis said firmly. "Please have a seat in the waiting room. I'll call you when the doctor is ready for you."

She turned before he could respond and walked behind the waiting-room counter.

He stared at the woman's broad back. Dammit. He was the one who was supposed to give the commands around here. Nevertheless, he turned and headed back to the waiting room, then sat stiffly on one of the leather-and-chrome armchairs.

Mavis sat at her computer and began typing. He was considering rushing the exam-room door when Liam came into the office, a cup of steaming coffee in his hand and a worried expression on his face. Mavis glanced up at the driver, gave him a stiff nod, then turned back to her computer.

Good, Dylan thought. Reinforcements.

"How is the lass?" Liam held out the coffee to Dylan, but he shook his head.

"I can't get past Attila to find out," Dylan muttered under his breath. "I could use a little diversion."

Liam grinned. "My specialty."

"Mavis, me darlin'." Liam sauntered over to the woman and leaned across the counter. "The wife's been asking why you haven't been to quilting circle.''

Mavis eyed him suspiciously. ''I've never been to quilting circle, Liam McNeil. Clair knows that.''

Liam scratched his neck and frowned. ''Maybe it was the gardening club, then, or was it—''

The cup of coffee in Liam's hand tumbled over the edge of the counter and exploded across Mavis's desk. With something between a shriek and a roar, Mavis jumped up, grabbed a box of tissues on her desk and blotted at the mess. When Liam came around to help, Dylan ducked past them both and headed down the hall.

He knocked lightly, heard ''Come in,'' then opened the door and stepped inside.

Wearing a light-blue gown, she sat on the edge of an examination table. Her legs and feet were bare and the sight of the scrapes and bruises on her knee and down her left leg made Dylan's chest tighten. She glanced up when he closed the door behind him and her eyes widened in surprise.

''I thought you were the nurse,'' she said, wrapping her arms protectively around her waist.

''She's been detained and asked me to come check on you.'' Dylan moved closer, winced at the blossoming bruise on the woman's cheek.

''Nurse Mavis asked you to check on me?''

''Well, not exactly,'' Dylan fessed up. ''I ordered three of the palace guards to tie her up so I could slip past her.''

A smile lurked at the corners of her mouth, then she glanced down and shook her head. ''I'm so sorry for all the trouble I've caused you. You've every right to be angry with me for being so careless."

"If I were angry, believe me, you would know. For that matter, the entire palace would know." He glanced at the top of her head, saw a small white butterfly strip covering the gash above her hairline. "Stitches?"

"No. Dr. Waltham said it should heal all right without any."

Gently, he took her chin in his hand, then tilted her face up. He saw the pain in her smoky-green eyes and had to bite back the swear word threatening to erupt. "How are you feeling?"

"Fine."

"Liar."

Her gaze dropped from his, her thick, dark lashes like a fan against her pale cheek. "I—I do feel as if I missed the top step of a tall staircase. The doctor gave me something for the pain a few minutes ago."

He knew he should remove his hand from her chin, but he lingered there a moment longer. Her skin was soft and smooth in his callused palm, ivory-white against his tanned fingers. But when his gaze strayed to her lips, when his pulse jumped, he released her and stepped back. "Where is the doctor?"

"He's looking at the X rays. He should be back any minute." She glanced up again. "Prince Dylan, I mean, Your Royal Highness—"

"Just call me Dylan." He hated the damn titles, hated that people treated him with such formality once they knew who he was. That was the one thing he'd enjoyed most these past two years. He'd been accepted by others for himself, not for his royal blood. "I still don't know what to call you, though. Have you remembered your name?"

She hugged her arms tightly to her. "No."

"Well, then." Dylan stared thoughtfully at her. "I suppose we'll have to try a few and see if anything rings a bell. Agnes?"

"I look like an Agnes?"

"Maybe not. Hortense?"

She lifted a brow.

"No, of course not. Gertrude?"

Dylan saw the amusement in her eyes as she shook her head.

"Irma? Sibyl? Chloe? Cornelia—"

"How about Emily?"

Dylan turned at the sound of a voice as Dr. Waltham entered the room. He stood at the open doorway, a file folder in one hand and a stern-looking Mavis Weidermeyer behind him. The white-haired doctor moved toward his patient, then held up something small between his thumb and index finger. The ruby ring she'd been wearing earlier, Dylan realized.

"We took it off when we cleaned up the scrapes on your hand," Dr. Waltham said. "There's an inscription inside the band, though we needed a magnifying glass to read it."

Her breath held, the woman stared at the ring, then looked back up at the doctor and whispered, "An inscription?"

"'To my dearest Emily.'" Dr. Waltham pressed the ring into her hand. "Though it doesn't mean for certain that's your name, I'm afraid until we find out more about you, Emily it is. Unless you have an objection, of course.''

"No. I—'' Her eyes moistened as she stared at the ring, then she slipped it on her finger. "Emily is fine.''

"The bad news is you've lost your memory, but amnesia following a trauma and blow of the sort you've had isn't out of the realm of normality. More than likely you'll slowly regain all the bits and pieces you've forgotten over the next few days or weeks.'' Dr. Waltham smiled. "The good news is that nothing is broken and I see no signs of serious injuries. You may have a mild concussion, though, and your shoulder has a nasty pull. I'm going to keep you overnight in the infirmary so we can monitor you, then a couple of days' rest should heal up your body well enough.''

"A few days?'' Emily put a hand to her temple. "But I can't stay here, I don't even—''

She started to sway and Dylan rushed toward her, held firmly on to her shoulders so she wouldn't fall off the table. She'd reached out instinctively and held on to his arms. Gently he eased her onto her back. She blinked several times, then her gaze steadied and met his. Her cheeks had paled even more, making the bruise on her face bloom brighter.

"Are you all right?'' he asked softly.

"Yes.'' Her hands tightened, then slid from his arms. "I'm sorry. I just got dizzy for a moment. I'll be fine.''

Dr. Waltham stepped beside Dylan. "I'm sure it's the pain pills, but let me have a look, anyway.''

Reluctantly, Dylan moved away while the doctor examined his patient. Mavis pulled a blanket from a corner cabinet and draped it over the younger woman, then lifted Emily's wrist and took her pulse.

Dylan stood by, helpless, watching as the doctor shone a tiny flashlight in Emily's eyes, then asked her to follow his finger without moving her head.

The doctor patted Emily's hand, then turned back to Dylan. "She just needs to rest now. We'll move her to a bed and you can—"

"I'll have the guest chamber next to my suite prepared for her."

"Your Royal Highness." Dr. Waltham furrowed his brow. "That's really not nec—"

In a tone Dylan rarely used with anyone, a tone that brooked no argument and no discussion, he said, "She'll be more comfortable in a real bed. You can send someone to monitor her there if it's necessary. Whatever you need, whatever she needs, take care of it."

Without looking back, he strode toward the door and walked out of the office.

Emily, if that was her name, was his responsibility now. And in spite of what people thought, in spite of what people said, Dylan Penwyck had never turned his back on an obligation or duty.

She woke to the smell of gardenias and the soft haze of early-morning light. Emily buried her face deeper into the marshmallow-soft pillow, not quite ready to give up the comfort of sleep. A dream, she thought, please let all this be a dream.

And please don't let me wake up.

But the distant rumble of thunder and the steady drip of rain off the eaves outside the bedroom window reminded her that it was not a dream at all. She truly was inside Penwyck Palace, snuggled under a thick down comforter that covered a four-poster canopied bed which was in and of itself fit for a king.

She barely remembered being brought here yesterday. The pain medication had not only eased her aches and pains, but had made her fall into a deep sleep for the night. Obviously the medication had worn off, she thought when she rolled to her back and her shoulder twanged in protest. Wincing, she lifted a hand to her forehead and pressed her fingers to the insistent, dull ache in her skull.

When the pain eased, she drew in a slow breath, then rose on one elbow and glanced around the spacious room. *Elegant* was her first thought, *Victorian romantic* was her second as she took in the canopied bed, lace curtains, floral wallpaper and a French country armoire.

And flowers. Beautiful long-stemmed pink roses, white carnations, purple delphiniums, all in a huge, cut-crystal vase on a round corner table. Beside the bed, pale-yellow Old English roses spilled from the sides of a clear glass bowl. Next to the roses, in a shallow porcelain dish, were two pure-white gardenias.

Tears burned Emily's eyes as she stared at the fragrant flowers. Everyone had been so nice to her since yesterday. Liam, Dr. Waltham, even Nurse

Weidermeyer, though Emily had to admit the woman did frighten her a bit.

And Dylan. In the back of the limo he'd been so incredibly gentle, then at the infirmary those piercing blue eyes of his had shown such concern. When he'd touched her chin so tenderly, her heart had skipped a beat. The texture of his callused hands on her skin had been electric. She'd almost forgotten she was sitting before him practically naked under the infirmary gown, had nearly forgotten where she was and why.

She hated that he'd blamed himself, even though she'd been the one to cause the accident. If only there was some way to undo what had been done, she thought as she stared at the sheer white canopy over her head, some way to turn back the clock and make things right.

But there wasn't, of course. She couldn't change a thing now. It was too late. She couldn't look back, knew she had no choice but to move forward.

At the sound of a soft knock at the door, Emily attempted to sit, but the effort sent a jolt of pain through her shoulder. With a gasp, she lay back against the pillows and struggled to find her voice.

"Come in."

The door opened slowly, and a rail-thin brunette wearing a gray-and-white maid's uniform wheeled a food cart into the room. The smell of peppermint tea and bacon reminded Emily that she hadn't eaten since the day before.

"Mornin' Miss Emily," the maid said cheerfully

and pushed the cart beside the bed. "My name is Sally. I hope I didn't wake you."

"No." Emily bit her lip and slowly, carefully, attempted to sit. "I was already awake."

"Let me help you." Sally quickly moved beside the bed and reached for another pillow, then slipped it behind Emily's back. "Your nurse went off to get your medication, and the doctor will be here in a little while to see how you're doing. Do you need to use the bathroom?"

"Not just yet." Emily let the worst of the pain pass, then forced a smile. "Please don't fuss over me. It's really not necessary."

"Oh, but it is, Miss Emily." Sally drew her brows together in a serious frown, then she turned and lifted the silver dome on a plate. Steam rose from a fluffy mound of scrambled eggs and several slices of bacon. "Not that I wouldn't want to fuss over you anyway, of course, but Prince Dylan was quite firm in his instructions."

Sally lifted a blue linen napkin covering a silver basket. Emily's mouth watered at the pile of pastries inside. "Instructions?"

"He said that you were to have anything you wanted, anything at all." Sally poured tea from a silver pot into a white china cup. "He also said if there was any problem, no matter how small, he was to be personally and immediately informed. Would you like cream in your tea?"

"Ah, no, thank you." Emily shifted until she found a comfortable spot, then accepted the tea Sally offered. "But surely Dyl—Prince Dylan—has more important matters to deal with than me."

Pulling out a wooden bed tray from underneath the cart, Sally placed it over Emily's legs, then reached for a set of silverware and a linen napkin. "Well, the palace has been in a bit of a bumble since King Morgan fell ill."

"The king is ill?"

"Heavens, yes. Very ill, with encephalitis, we were told. We're all so happy he's out of danger now and recovering. It's been a huge relief for the queen and Prince Owen that Prince Dylan has finally come home."

Emily sipped the tea Sally handed her; the warmth of the liquid relaxed her. "Prince Dylan has been gone?"

"You don't know?" Sally stared at Emily in bewilderment, then, with a small gasp, pressed her hand to her mouth. "I was told that you've lost your memory, but I wasn't thinking. So it's true, then? You really don't remember anything? Who you are or where you're from?"

The ache in Emily's temple became a throb at Sally's question. Closing her eyes, she simply shook her head.

"Oh dear, I'm so sorry I've upset you." Distressed, the maid wrung her hands. "Here I am, supposed to take care of you and I'm only making things worse."

"No." Emily drew in a long breath, then opened her eyes again and forced a smile. "No. You've done nothing. Tell me about Prince Dylan."

Sally's face took on a dreamy look. "Prince Dylan is…amazing."

Emily tried not to smile. It appeared that the young maid had a crush on Dylan. Not that Emily was surprised. What woman under eighty wouldn't be swooning over the handsome prince? Hadn't she found her own stomach fluttering when he'd touched her?

"You said he'd been gone," Emily prompted.

"For nearly two years." Sally set the plate of bacon and eggs on the tray. "No one knows exactly where he's been or what he's been doing. Some say he was in Africa, hunting dangerous animals in the thickest, darkest jungles. Some say he was at sea, sailing the vast, endless oceans, visiting the most exotic ports and women. There's even talk of an Italian contessa and a secluded villa." Sally paused with a sigh. "He's quite the ladies' man, you know. So rugged and handsome and a smile that would make any woman melt on the spot."

"I'm sure there are puddles all around the world," Emily said dryly, more than a little unnerved that she'd had exactly the same reaction to the man.

"There are other rumors, too." Sally leaned closer and whispered, "But so outrageous I really don't think I should repeat them."

"No," Dylan said stiffly from the doorway as he stepped into the room. Annoyance narrowed his eyes. "You really shouldn't."

Three

"**P**rince Dylan!" Her face bright red, Sally spun around and curtsied awkwardly. "I—I thought you were in a meeting with Admiral Monteque this morning."

Dylan resisted the urge to tug at the charcoal silk tie around his neck, wished to God he didn't have to wear these damn suits to informal meetings. "Not for another hour."

Completely flustered that she'd been caught talking about a member of the royal family, an offense that she knew she could be fired for, the young maid began to babble. "I—I'm sorry, Your Royal Highness. I didn't mean to, that is, I wouldn't have—"

"Never mind, Sally." Frowning, Dylan waved a dismissive hand. "I'd like to speak to Emily, if you don't mind."

Sally folded her hands in front of her and smiled. "Well, of course I don't mind."

Dylan lifted a brow. "Alone."

"Oh, yes, of course, of course. I'm so sorry." The maid pushed the food cart aside, then glanced at Emily. "I'll be back in a little while to help you with a bath and wash your hair, but if you need anything at all, just dial two-four on the phone. Or I can wait outside, if you like, or I can—"

"*Sally.*"

The maid jumped at Dylan's sharp reprimand, then backed toward the door, her eyes cast downward as she bowed out of the room.

Brow furrowed, Dylan stared at the closed door for a long moment. He'd never quite gotten used to the bows and curtsies he'd been subjected to his entire life. He'd accepted all the formality as part of his inherited duty, but still, that didn't mean he had to like it.

There were times he was thankful that his brother would be named the next king. From the time they'd been young children, Owen had been more suited to rule Penwyck. He'd always had more patience, more interest in the politics of the country, while Dylan had found it difficult to stay in one place for any length of time or to follow the endless rules that the royal family was subject to. And his temper had gotten him in trouble on more than one occasion, a fact that his mother had lamented over his entire life.

And still, there were times that Dylan wondered if he could make a difference if he were to rule the country, if he could curb his temper and rule with his intellect instead of his emotions.

But what did it matter? Owen would be the next king of Penwyck, and Dylan bore his twin no ill will over that fact. Owen would make a fine king. He had a wife, Jordan, who would be a lovely queen, and their four-year-old daughter, Whitney, was already a beautiful princess. Owen would make their parents and family and all the people of Penwyck proud.

Dylan turned his attention to Emily. Pillows plumped behind her back, she sat upright in the large bed, a breakfast tray perched across her legs. She watched him with a cautious, uncertain expression in her eyes, eyes still glazed and heavy from sleep.

His blood stirred at the sight of her. With her thick, dark hair tumbling around her pale face and slender shoulders, and the soft rise of her bare breasts at the V of her green silk pajama top, she seemed more fantasy than reality.

Then his gaze dropped to the mark on her cheek and reality returned. A swear word hovered on the tip of his tongue, but he checked himself before it escaped. Though the swelling appeared less noticeable than the day before, the bruise itself had darkened to an angry, deep blue.

"Good morning, Your Royal Highness." She lifted her gaze to his when he moved beside the bed. "I hope you'll forgive me if I don't curtsy. You've caught me at a disadvantage, I'm afraid."

"From where I'm standing, Emily, you are hardly what I, or any other man, would consider disadvantaged." Her blush spread across her cheeks and

down the long, smooth column of her neck. Once
again his gaze was drawn to her breasts, and he saw
the outline of her nipples under the thin silk pajama
top. The blood she'd stirred only a moment ago now
began to heat quickly.

Forcing his mind off ravaging the woman, Dylan
cleared his throat. "How are you feeling?"

"As if my head were a forest," she replied. "And
a little man with a chain saw is busy cutting down
the trees."

He reached for the phone. "I'll have your nurse
paged right away."

"It's just a headache." She touched his arm to
stop him, then quickly pulled away. "I'm sorry,
Your Royal Highness. That was presumptuous of me
and I—"

"Stop that." He frowned at her, then pulled the
chair from beside the nightstand next to the bed and
sat down. With a sigh, he took her hand in his. "Emily, I told you yesterday, when we're alone, I'd
rather you call me Dylan."

"I—" She dropped her gaze. "If you like."

"I like."

He liked a lot of things when it came to Emily,
Dylan realized. The lovely flush of pink on her
cheeks, the soft lilt of her voice, her calm courage.
Most of the women he'd known would have been in
hysterics over all that had happened and would probably have the entire palace staff running in ten different directions.

But Emily had asked for nothing, had even
seemed embarrassed over all the attention. Though

that told him a lot about her character, he still knew nothing of who she actually was, or her background.

He closed his hand around hers. Her fingers were warm today, and he wondered if she was as smooth and soft all over. When he lightly brushed her wrist with his thumb, he felt her pulse jump under his touch. "Have you remembered anything?"

He saw the anguish in her eyes before she closed them and turned her head away. Dammit! Dylan cursed himself for pressing her. Dr. Waltham had warned him yesterday how stressful amnesia—even partial amnesia—was to a person. She was already in enough pain, and the last thing she needed right now was a lot of questions she couldn't answer.

He'd know soon enough, anyway. He'd already asked Pierceson Prescott to look into the matter for him. Dylan was certain it wouldn't be long before the respected member of King Morgan's Royal Elite Team discovered this woman's identity. It wasn't as if she'd dropped out of the sky, after all.

Oddly, Dylan hoped that it wouldn't be *too* soon. He knew that when she found out who she was, who her family was, she would be gone. It was hard to admit, but he wasn't ready to let go of the lovely Emily just yet.

"Eat." He released her hand and gestured to the food on the tray. "Chef Boudreau is one of the few luxuries I missed while I was away. The man is a genius."

She picked up the cup and sipped at it. "Maybe just the tea."

"Food." Dylan reached for a fork and stabbed a

bite of egg, then held it to her lips. "No argument, and that's an order."

"An order, is it?" She lifted a brow. "I thought you were just Dylan when we were alone."

"That depends on how cooperative you are." He felt his heart jump when her mouth closed over the fork. When he scooped up another bite of egg, the smile in her eyes faded.

"Dylan," she said softly and took the fork from him. "I can feed myself, thank you. Maybe if you ate something, too, I wouldn't feel so self-conscious."

To make her more comfortable, he plucked a scone from her tray and sat back in his chair. The rain had eased up, and the steady *drip drip drip* off the eaves was the only sound in the room.

She ate delicately, tiny little bites, and each time she lifted the fork to her lips, Dylan felt a tightening in his groin. He knew he should look away. Lusting after a woman who lay injured and in pain was hardly a gentlemanly thing to do, especially when he'd been the one to inflict the injuries.

But then, he hadn't always claimed to be a gentleman.

"Sally told me you've been away from the palace for two years," Emily said after a few moments. "That's a long time to be away from your family. You must have missed them very much."

"Yes." He hadn't realized how much until he'd returned. "Though my sisters have been horrible nags about how long I'd been gone and the fact I'd been hard to reach."

"So was it the jungle, the ocean or the Italian villa?"

"What?"

"I'm sorry." Reaching for her napkin, she dabbed at the corners of her mouth. "I shouldn't have asked that."

"Ah. The rumors." He lifted his chin. "I've heard the jungle and ocean ones, but the Italian villa?"

She cast a sideways glance at him. "Where you've been hiding out while you were gone, with your lover, the contessa."

Dylan couldn't remember that he'd ever been with the same woman for two weeks, let alone two years. "Oh, *that* villa," he said, taking another bite of scone. "I'd forgotten. There have been so many."

Emily raised a brow. "Villas or women?"

"Rumors."

Too many, Dylan thought in annoyance. From the time he was seventeen, the paparazzi and media had lurked in shadows and hidden around corners everywhere he'd gone. If he had so much as glanced at a woman, suddenly they were a couple, deeply in love, with eyes only for each other. According to the tabloids, Dylan Penwyck had been secretly engaged or actually married more times than he could count. His personal favorite was the eyewitness who'd sworn to have seen him in a Las Vegas chapel, slipping a ring on a famous model's hand while an Elvis minister presided over the ceremony.

Still, he hadn't much cared what the newspapers reported one way or the other, even when the headlines had been less than admirable. The only one that had ever bothered him in the slightest had been the accusation he'd fathered a baby and left his lover in poverty and rags while he dined in the finest restaurant with three buxom blondes then got into a drunken brawl with a waiter.

He still saw red every time he thought of that article and the accompanying photograph that barely resembled him. No Penwyck man would *ever* turn his back on his own child, let alone leave them in poverty.

It was the only time Dylan had personally stepped in and insisted on an apology, written and public, then made a "suggestion" to the newspaper that they make a rather large contribution to a local social services agency that assisted single pregnant women and mothers.

"I'm sorry," Dylan heard Emily say quietly. "I've upset you."

Dylan turned his attention back to the woman in the bed. She watched him with a worried look in her green eyes, and the sight of her lying there, so fragile and delicate, made him forget about the irritation he'd felt over that damn tabloid article.

Smiling, he shook his head. "Rumors go with the territory, I'm afraid. But it's certainly taught me that you can't believe everything you read, or even what you hear and see. Things," he said evenly, "are not always what they seem."

Her expression was blank as she held his gaze. "Prince Dylan is a cynic?"

"I question," he said, then leaned close. "Especially when it comes to beautiful young women with amnesia.''

He caught the slight intake of her breath before she replied, ''Are you complimenting me, Your Highness, or cross-examining?''

''Dylan,'' he reminded her. ''And if I have to tell you it's a compliment, then I *have* been in the jungle for too long.''

''Ah.'' She arched a brow. ''So you *were* in the jungle, then?''

He shrugged. ''Jungle, ocean, villa. Las Vegas wedding chapel.'' He smiled at the curious lift of her brow. ''What difference does it make? I'm home now, that's all that matters. My family and serving my country are all that are important to me now.''

Emily glanced away, but not before he saw the tears suddenly form in her eyes. He tucked a finger under her chin, then turned her face back toward him.

''I'm sorry,'' he said quietly. ''It must be hard for you, not knowing if your own family is out there somewhere, looking for you, wondering if you're all right.''

''I—'' She paused, swallowed hard. ''I couldn't bear it if I thought any harm had come to someone I loved.''

A tear dropped on his hand. He stared at that single drop of moisture, then frowned at the unexpected hitch in his chest. A woman's tears had never affected him so. Had never inspired him to comfort or soothe.

Pulling his hand away from her, he stood quickly,

then forced himself to slip into the stance he reserved for formal public occasions. "You should rest now. Nurse Mavis will have me drawn and quartered if I overtax her patient. If you need anything at all, dial zero and you'll be connected with the proper department."

"Thank you." She lifted her gaze to his. "You've been more than kind."

He turned, was nearly to the door when she called his name. He glanced over his shoulder.

"What if I need you?" she asked softly.

Dylan felt his blood heat, then surge through his veins. Too stunned to speak for a moment, he simply stared at her.

Blushing, she said quickly, "I mean, if I need to speak with you?"

"Star twenty-four will page me." He swallowed the dryness in his throat. "Star twenty-five will put you through to the private phone in my suite."

He didn't give her a chance to answer, just left, nearly closed the doors on his own heels in his hurry to get out before he did or said something he knew he'd regret.

"This chartreuse linen was absolutely *made* for you, Emily. With your hair and your coloring, you'll be nothing short of *fantastic*. Oh, let's try it on."

Emily bit the inside of her mouth, swearing if she heard those four little words—*let's try it on*—one more time, she might scream. Devonna Demetrius, a short-haired platinum blonde who was the most recent addition to the staff of palace couturieres, had shown up at Emily's bedside two hours ago, followed by a large, rolling rack of clothes that ranged from sportswear to evening gowns. There were trays underneath overflowing with lingerie and mountains of boxes filled with shoes.

Yesterday, a simple phone call from Dylan had set Operation Wardrobe in motion. Devonna, assistant to Princess Megan's couturiere, had spent most of the previous day in Emily's room with a measuring tape in one hand and a color chart in the other. The couturiere had been given free rein with Prince Dylan's charge, and though Emily had insisted that a few simple items were all she needed, Devonna would hear nothing of it.

If Prince Dylan ordered a new wardrobe for Emily, then Emily—whether she wanted one or not—would have a new wardrobe.

Devonna practically quivered with pleasure over the carte blanche she'd been given. Emily couldn't help but think that the assistant couturiere was like a wiry terrier who'd been given a meaty bone—Emily herself being the meaty bone.

Dylan had left strict instructions with the staff that his guest was to be taken care of. Emily might have felt as if a hockey team had used her for a puck, but she wasn't crippled, for heaven's sake. She was feeling much better today. She didn't need Sally to draw a bath for her, or warm the towels or wash and blow-dry her hair. She didn't need Nurse Mavis sternly standing watch all day, taking her pulse and blood pressure and asking her how she felt.

And she certainly didn't need an entire wardrobe,

either, she thought, glancing at all the beautiful clothes. She couldn't keep any of these things. When this was over, she would dress in her own clothes, which had already been cleaned and mended and now hung in the closet, and she would leave.

But Devonna's determination and enthusiasm had worn Emily down. That, and the fact that it was late in the day and she simply hadn't the strength or energy to argue with the woman any longer.

"Miss Demetrius—"

"Dee Dee." Devonna carefully slipped the jacket up Emily's arms and onto her shoulders, rushed around to examine her creation, then pushed her oversized black-rimmed glasses up her nose. "Omigod, it's *perfect*. Will you just *look* at yourself? Wait, wait, let me get the heels."

"Dee Dee, I don't need a linen jacket and skirt." Still, while the zealous woman dug through a pile of shoe boxes, Emily glanced at the trio of full-length mirrors in the corner of the large dressing room attached to the bathroom.

It *was* perfect, Emily thought with a sigh. Everything Dee Dee had brought had been wonderful—a variety of conservative and youthful, fun and sophisticated. What woman wouldn't be thrilled with such an abundance of beautiful, expensive clothes?

Dee Dee yanked a pair of white walking shoes from a box, frowned, then tossed them aside. "Darn," she muttered to herself as she pushed her glasses up her nose again. "I know they're here somewhere."

While Dee Dee continued to mutter to herself and

dig through more boxes, Emily sank down on a softly cushioned tapestry-covered armchair. Elegance and luxury surrounded her, from the plush, deep-blue carpet under her bare feet, to the white marble counter and gold-framed mirrors.

She didn't deserve this kindness and generosity, Emily thought miserably. She hated this attention, hated being fussed over. She looked at her reflection in the mirrors, barely recognized the bruised face that stared back at her in triplicate.

Liar.

The word pounded inside her head like a hammer, and she closed her eyes against the pain. Liar. Cheat. Fraud. She was all that and worse.

Two days ago, when she'd still been at the infirmary and Dylan had come in to check on her in the examination room, it had taken every last ounce of willpower she possessed to hold herself together, to remain strong. Yesterday, when he'd joined her for breakfast, and again this morning, he'd been so attentive, so concerned, she'd nearly crumbled completely.

Her hatred for the people, the *animals,* who'd forced her to do this despicable thing grew with every breath she took. Never in her life had she felt so helpless, so utterly powerless.

Six days ago, she'd been at home in West County, busy grading papers for her first-grade class, waiting for her grandmother to come home from afternoon tea in the village. Then the phone had rung and Emily had picked up the call, changing her life forever.

"If you do exactly what we say," a man had whis-

pered at the other end of the line, *"no harm will come to your grandmother."*

Fear, like ice-cold fingers, slid up Emily's spine. Her hand had tightened on the receiver. A joke, this had to be a bad joke. "Who is this?" she'd demanded.

"You don't need to know that." His voice was deep, threatening. *"You only need to do what you're told."*

"Where is my grandmother?" Emily insisted. *"Tell me this instant or I'll call the police and—"*

"You'll call no one," he had said with deadly calm. *"You'll tell no one. If you do, your grandmother will meet with a fatal accident."*

Oh, God. This couldn't be happening. It couldn't be. What would anyone want with her, or her grandmother?

"There has to be a mistake," she said weakly. *"You must have the wrong person."*

"You are Emily Bridgewater. Your grandmother is Olivia Bridgewater. We need you to do something for us, Emily. We'll take good care of your grandmother until you do."

We? Who could these people be? And what could they possibly need her for?

"I am going to put your grandmother on the phone now," the man said. *"You will pretend that everything is fine, and that you'll be joining her as soon as you can."*

"I don't understand, please just—"

"Ah, Olivia, there you are, my dear." The man's voice suddenly became loud and extremely friendly.

"I have Emily on the phone now. She'd like to say hello to you."

"Emily, what a darling you are to surprise me with such a wonderful gift," her grandmother said brightly. *"The resort is so luxurious and everyone is so kind. Especially Frederick, why he's barely left my side, the dear man."*

"Grandmother—" Emily fought back the panic *"—are you all right?"*

"Well, of course I am, dear. How could I not be fine, in such a wonderful place? I—"

The line went dead.

Her knees too weak to hold her, Emily sank to the floor. The walls of the small house she shared with her grandmother began to spin around her. When the phone rang again, her hand shook so badly she'd nearly dropped the receiver. A different man at the other end told her what she needed to do, then arranged a meeting.

After she'd hung up the phone, Emily had run to the bathroom and thrown up.

Olivia Bridgewater was the only family Emily had left. She'd only been seventeen when her father had been killed in a mining accident, then she'd lost her mother three years later to cancer. Her grandmother, at seventy-three, was as spry and healthy as ever, but her sense of time and place was often confused.

Emily loved her grandmother more than life itself. If any harm came to her, Emily wouldn't be able to bear it.

She had no choice but to do what these thugs told her to do, but when her grandmother was safely returned, she swore she'd do everything in her power to have the men caught and punished.

"Here they are!"

Startled out of her thoughts by the couturiere's excited declaration, Emily felt her heart slam against her ribs. She grabbed on to the sides of the chair, forced herself to take slow, deep breaths.

"These will be per—" High-heels in hand, Dee Dee was turning when she caught sight of Emily. The shoes fell to the floor. "Oh, God. You're pale as a ghost. I'll go ring for your nurse."

"No." Emily took hold of Dee Dee's arm before she could leave. "I'm fine. Really. I'm just a little tired."

"I've done too much, haven't I?" Frowning, Dee Dee rushed to Emily's side. "I'm so sorry. Here, let's get this off and get you back in bed."

Emily stood, dropped her arms to her sides as Dee Dee slid the jacket off her shoulders, then the skirt down her legs. Wearing nothing but a lace-edged, white silk slip with built-in bra, Emily stood in the middle of the dressing room while the couturiere tore through the lingerie trays, looking for a fresh pair of pajamas.

A knock from the outer room had them both turning. Dee Dee shoved her glasses up her nose, then gently took Emily by the shoulders and eased her back down into the chair. "I'll be right back. Don't move."

As soon as the woman rounded the corner, Emily stood and took a step toward the rack of clothes. When the dizziness overtook her, she sat down on the carpet, pressed her fingers to her temples and closed her eyes.

"Emily, you've got—oh!"

Emily heard the distress in Dee Dee's voice, tried to tell the couturiere that she'd simply stood up too quickly, but she couldn't quite get the words out.

In the next second, a pair of strong arms came around her and lifted her off the floor. His mouth set in a thin line, Dylan held her close.

"Go find Mavis."

Four

"Dylan, please, put me down. I'm fine."

"Unless you were practicing a yoga position down there," Dylan said tightly, "I'd say you aren't fine at all."

It surprised him that he wasn't feeling so fine himself, that his nerves were a little shaky at the sight of Emily sitting on the floor in her slip, her legs twisted underneath her. Under normal circumstances, Dylan never would have barged into a lady's dressing room, but when he'd heard the couturiere's gasp of surprise, he hadn't thought about what was proper.

"I got up too quickly and had a little head rush, so I sat down." Emily laid a hand on his chest. "There's absolutely nothing wrong with me."

To look at her, Dylan would have to agree. The

silk slip she wore didn't cover much, and in spite of the situation, he indulged himself and let his gaze roam over her. Her feet were small, her toenails painted baby pink. His eyes slid up her long, smooth legs; noticed the scrapes on her knee were starting to heal. Unable to stop himself, he followed the seam between her firm thighs upward to where soft, creamy skin met lace.

His throat went instantly dry; heat surged through his veins. And when he glanced up at her breasts, cupped in soft white lace and pressing firmly against his chest, all the blood from the upper part of his body shot to his groin.

The scent of lavender drifted from her warm skin. Her face, only inches from his, flushed with color. He couldn't have moved if his life had depended on it, so he stood there, her soft body in his arms. Her hand lay lightly on his chest, and he was certain she felt the swift beating of his heart under her palm.

When her eyes, those smoke-filled green eyes, lifted to his, he went instantly hard.

"I'm taking you to bed," Dylan murmured. He watched her eyes widen at his words, heard the soft catch of her breath. He turned and walked to her bed, set her down on the soft mattress, then startled them both by brushing his lips against hers. "The next time I tell you I'm taking you to bed, Emily, it will mean something entirely different."

"Dylan, I—"

"What's happened?" Nurse Mavis stormed into the room with Dee Dee in tow. "Stand back, let me have a look at her."

Dylan stepped away, watched the expression in Emily's eyes shift from aroused to anxious. "I'm fine, really. You needn't—"

"Miss Demetrius!" Mavis frowned darkly at the couturiere. "Get Miss Emily a robe immediately."

Dee Dee rushed to the dressing room while Mavis checked Emily for any signs of injury or shock. When Sally burst into the room, the bedroom turned into a frenetic beehive of activity. Even while Emily kept insisting that she was all right, the women buzzed around her, tucking her under the covers, fanning her, filling a glass of water.

He should have left the women to their ministrations; he certainly had no business standing around a woman's boudoir while the staff attended to her. She wasn't his wife, wasn't even his lover.

Yet.

Decisions had always been easy for Dylan. From the time he was young, he'd had the ability to assess a person or a situation quickly and thoroughly, then determine a course of action. He'd fine-tuned that ability over these past two years. His assignments with Graystroke had forced him to make split-second life-or-death decisions. He'd had to learn to think fast and listen to his gut. Every decision hadn't always been the right one, there were risks in life. He accepted that, and his mistakes, then moved on.

Emily might very likely be one of those risks, one of those mistakes. Nevertheless, he'd made his decision. He wanted her.

And he intended to have her.

Clearly, she was attracted to him as well, though

she hadn't flirted or blatantly come on to him the way most women did when they were interested. If anything, she'd done her best to hide her interest, which might have made him think she was being coy. But he'd felt her tremble in his arms, had seen the look in her eyes and recognized it: desire.

He hadn't figured the woman out yet, which should have been all the more reason to keep his distance. He knew there was something under the surface with Emily, something he couldn't put his finger on. It wasn't so much that he thought she was lying, as that he felt she was avoiding the truth. It made him wary, but it certainly didn't discourage him. If anything, he thought, it only intrigued him all the more. The uncertainty, the challenge, aroused more than his interest.

"Please." Pressing her hands to her temple, Emily sat abruptly. "*Please*. There's nothing wrong with me."

Still, the women persisted. Miss Demetrius was unfolding a fresh pair of white silk pajamas, Sally was attempting to clip Emily's thick hair up on her head and Mavis was taking her pulse.

Emily glanced at Dylan, her gaze pleading. He was about to step forward and pull rank, when another voice, a familiar feminine one, stopped him.

"What in the world is going on in here?"

All heads turned, then everyone froze.

Confused by the sudden shift in the room's climate, Emily peeked from around Mavis's large frame. When she saw who had entered, Emily forgot to breathe.

Queen Marissa stood in the doorway. The woman was as stunningly beautiful in person as she was on television and in all the photographs Emily had ever seen of her. Her eyes were a striking blue, much like Dylan's, and though she was in her early fifties, she looked younger and carried her tall, slim figure with elegance and sophistication. She wore a jacket and skirt of royal blue, and her dark, straight hair had been swept up on top of her head.

Dylan nodded to his mother as she entered the room. The women—including Mavis—quickly curtsied.

Emily clasped a hand to her throat. She still hadn't recovered from Dylan pressing his lips to hers and now the *queen*—Queen Marissa—was right here in her bedroom! She had no idea what to do, what was appropriate or not. She started to slip out of bed to curtsy, as well, but the queen raised a hand.

"Stay where you are, my dear." Marissa glanced at the other women. "Leave us now, please."

The room was cleared in three seconds, with only Dylan, Queen Marissa and herself left.

Emily felt the prickle of perspiration under her arms. She'd never considered coming face-to-face with the queen, and the enormity of the situation left her speechless.

"Mother, may I introduce Emily to you?" Dylan stepped forward. His voice was formal and stiff. "Emily, my mother. Queen Marissa Penwyck."

"I—" Panic filled Emily. She dropped her gaze and nodded. "An honor to meet you, Your Majesty."

"Thank you." The queen moved closer to the bed. "How are you feeling this evening?"

"I'm much better, thank you." Emily resisted the temptation to duck under the covers. If Mavis were to take her pulse now, Emily thought, the nurse would probably insist her patient be admitted to ICU. "You've been so kind to allow me to stay here."

"We would hardly have left you in the road, Emily. Especially after running you down with the palace limousine. That would be most unseemly."

"Thank you, Your Majesty, but I am the only one to blame for the accident. I was careless."

Marissa lifted a finely arched brow. "It's not polite to argue with the queen."

"I—I'm sorry," Emily stumbled.

"She's teasing you, Emily," Dylan said gently, then gave his mother a half grin. "The queen does have a sense of humor on occasion."

"With three daughters, two sons and a husband like King Morgan, it's been essential." Queen Marissa smiled at Dylan. "The prince, on occasion, has one himself. Ask him about the time he strapped a tiny gold crown on a bullfrog and let it loose in his father's office."

The love between mother and son was obvious, Emily thought as she glanced from Dylan to Marissa, and couldn't help but think of her grandmother and how much she loved her. Though she knew that Olivia was being treated well, the thought of those horrible men harming her grandmother once again strengthened Emily's resolve.

She might not like what she'd been forced to do,

but until she could think of a way out of this, she simply had no choice.

"I'm sorry to hear about the king," Emily said hesitantly. "I do hope he's feeling better."

"He's out of danger now, thank you. He bellowed quite loudly when the doctor drew his blood this morning, a good sign that he's on the mend." Marissa turned her attention to her son. "Will you be joining the family for dinner this evening?"

Dylan shook his head. "We'll be finalizing the details of the alliance with Drogheda and Marjorco tonight. Owen has a conference scheduled with both ambassadors on Drogheda tomorrow."

"You'll not go with him?" Marissa asked.

"There's no need. Owen and I agreed that one of us should stay on Penwyck at all times."

"Perhaps."

It was odd, Emily thought, the fleeting glimpse of anxiety in the queen's expression, the hesitation in her voice. But it was gone just as quickly, then she stepped forward and placed a kiss on her son's cheek. "I'll have Chef Boudreau save a pastry for you. Goodnight, dear."

Emily's pulse jumped when the queen turned back to her. "Do take care, Emily. Do not hesitate to ask if you need anything at all."

Praying that her eyes did not reflect the guilt slicing through her heart, Emily dropped her gaze in a gesture of respect. "Thank you, Your Majesty."

"Perhaps if you're well enough tomorrow, you'd like a tour of the palace," Marissa said. "Princess

Megan and Princess Meredith are both excellent guides.''

Stop! Emily wanted say. Stop being so nice! ''I—I couldn't impose.''

''Nonsense.'' Marissa's voice brooked no argument. ''Sally will take care of your needs for an outing.''

Like a true queen, Marissa turned and swept from the room.

Emily stared after her for a long moment, blinking back the moisture burning her eyes. *I can do this,* she told herself and touched the ring on her finger, the ring her grandmother had given her. *I can.*

''Is everything all right?'' Dylan asked.

She heard the concern in his voice, knew that his kindness, everyone's kindness, would be her undoing. She lay back against the pillows and lowered her gaze, afraid if he looked into her eyes she would be lost. Her grandmother would be lost.

''It's been a long day,'' she said quietly.

''I'll leave you then.'' He moved closer and her pulse raced, pounded in her skull.

When he leaned closer still, she felt the heat of his body. He'd kissed her earlier, a simple, light brush of lips, yet not so simple at all. His mouth on hers had been electric and she'd felt her body respond with a will of its own.

The next time I tell you I'm taking you to bed he had said when he'd held her in his arms; *it will mean something entirely different.*

She hadn't the energy to resist him if he kissed her again. Her need for comfort, for reassurance, was too strong right now. She should be pleased that he was interested in her, wasn't that why she'd been sent here? To seduce him, to deceive him?

But there was no pleasure in knowing that he wanted her. How could there be, when she was such a fraud?

She felt him tug the comforter up to cover her shoulders, then squeezed her eyes tightly shut.

"Rest well, Emily," he said close to her ear. She shivered at the warm brush of his breath on her skin. "I'm anxious for you to heal quickly."

When she heard the door close softly a moment later, Emily let the tears slide down her face. Tears of anger, tears of frustration, tears of guilt.

She'd do what these vile men had insisted of her, and then she'd see each and every one of them rot in hell.

Fifteen men from King Morgan's Royal Intelligence Institute and the Royal Elite Team, plus Owen and Dylan, sat in black leather armchairs around the polished twenty-foot-long mahogany conference table. Oil paintings of previous Penwyck rulers and several famous dukes and prime ministers hung on ivory-colored walls. Crystal glasses, one before each chair, were filled with ice water, but coffee had been the drink of choice at the meeting and the silver carafes in the middle of the table were nearly empty. Servants had been allowed in the board room only to replenish coffee and water and a tray of assorted sandwiches.

With so many security breaches in the past few

months, including Owen's kidnapping and his sister Anastasia's near-fatal plane crash, precautions were being taken beyond the ordinary. Though the palace was still celebrating Penwyck's most recent alliance with the United States, there were two principalities, Drogheda and Marjorco, that were still haggling over details.

Dylan pinched the bridge of his nose with his thumb and forefinger and listened while Admiral Monteque, the head of the Penwyck Royal Navy, offered his suggestion on the disagreement over international waters, an important issue which Owen would be negotiating with the ambassadors to Drogheda and Marjorco at their conference over the next few days. If all went well, the alliances with both countries would be complete within the month.

Owen, who'd been sitting beside Dylan, stood at the conclusion of Admiral Monteque's discussion. "I believe we've covered everything on our agenda for the evening, gentlemen. Thank you all for being here. My father is recovering quickly and sends his regards to everyone."

Applause broke out at Owen's announcement. The king and his counsel had been greatly missed these past few months. There had been chaos since Morgan's twin brother, Broderick, had been brought in temporarily to run the kingdom, but since he'd been forced to step down two weeks earlier, order had slowly returned.

And Uncle Broderick, strangely enough, was nowhere to be found.

There'd been accusations that Dylan's uncle was

connected to the Black Knights, some even suggested
he was their leader. But there'd been no conclusive
proof so far. It was hard to believe that Broderick
could be aligned with a fanatical group of activists
whose sole purpose was to disrupt the government of
Penwyck, but Dylan knew it was certainly possible.
Broderick had been bitter that Morgan had been cho-
sen to rule Penwyck for the past thirty years. His bit-
terness might very well have aligned him with the
terrorist group.

But if Broderick was associated with the Black
Knights, Dylan was certain that he would be found
out. And the fact that he was King Morgan's brother
would only increase the man's punishment, not di-
minish it.

There would be no sympathy, no mercy for anyone
affiliated with the Black Knights.

"Excuse me, Your Royal Highness." Pierceson
Prescott approached Dylan while a few others milled
about the conference room. "May I speak with you?"

"Of course."

"You asked me to check on the woman your car
struck on the road," Pierceson said when he and Dylan stepped to a quiet corner.

Dylan nodded. "Emily."

"It appears that is her name," Pierceson said. "Her
bicycle was rented down in the village from a vendor
named Joseph Wellman. She signed a form that the
vendor requires for rentals, a waiver of responsibility
for accidents and a promise to return the bike in the
same condition it was rented."

Dylan's pulse jumped, though he kept his gaze on the other man steady. "And?"

"That's the problem." Pierceson shook his head. "There is no *and*. She simply signed her name *Emily*. She was alone when she rented the bike, and she paid cash. Told the man that she was off to sightsee and she'd return in a few hours."

Dylan frowned. "That's it?"

"The vendor admitted that he'd been interested in Emily, had asked her if her husband would be joining her. She'd told the man no, that she wasn't married. I'm checking the local areas for abandoned cars, and also the inns and hotels for guests who might match the woman's description."

So she's not married.

Relief, then pleasure surged through his veins, though Dylan kept his face blank while he listened to Prescott mention additional investigative procedures he'd put in place.

But even with this new information, Dylan realized, the lovely Emily was as big a mystery now as she had been before.

Five

It was one thing to read about the wealthy and privileged, Emily thought while she listened to Sally's tuneless humming from the dressing room. The money, the servants, private chefs and fancy clothes. But it was quite another thing to be a part of it, to actually be living the life most people only dreamed about. To be certain, it was wonderful, yet terrifying at the same time. Emily glanced down at the simple white cotton blouse and beige wool slacks she wore, knew that both articles of clothing bore the label of an internationally renowned designer.

And if that weren't enough, the chocolate-colored cashmere cardigan Dee Dee had insisted that Emily wear—heavens! Emily doubted that a week's paycheck teaching at the Clarton Elementary School would pay for the luxurious sweater. The entire outfit, complete with the kid-leather brown flats, would probably have cost Emily an entire month's salary.

With a sigh, she sat on the edge of the bed. She missed her children, all eighteen of them: little Darrin Donaldson, with his unruly red hair and endless questions; Edwina Barron, with her perfect ponytail and big blue eyes; Molly Gibson, whose infectious giggling disrupted the class constantly. Emily was sure they'd all be fine with a substitute teacher for a couple of weeks, and with the holiday break coming the week after next, Emily knew she wouldn't miss too much of the school year.

Unless something went wrong.

The knot already in her stomach tightened. Even if she did everything those awful men asked of her, even if she gave them the information they wanted, how did she know they still wouldn't kill her and her grandmother?

She couldn't know, of course. And it certainly wasn't as if she trusted them to honor their word. She'd tried to convince herself that they had no reason to harm anyone if she did what they said. After all, she was committing a crime. She could never tell anyone what she'd done. If she did, she would be put in jail herself. Then who would take care of her grandmother? Emily worried. Olivia's eyesight wasn't as good as it had been even last year, and sometimes she forgot to take her blood-pressure medication.

But there had been one thing, one precaution Emily had taken to protect her grandmother and herself.

If anything went wrong, she prayed that what had been a chance mistake would save their lives.

The night she'd received that first phone call, her answering machine had picked up at the same time she'd lifted the receiver. The entire conversation had been recorded. Everything that had been said was now on a microcassette, tucked away in a safe place. She knew it wouldn't keep her out of jail, but at the very least it might somehow prevent those men from deciding that they no longer wanted anyone living who could testify against them. That tape was her ace-in-the-hole. No one knew about it. She would tell no one until she'd completed what she'd come here to do. The tape was her bargaining chip to make certain she got her grandmother safely back and that no future "accidents" might happen.

For now, she needed to concentrate on why she was here and what she needed to do. Not an easy task, considering she couldn't stop thinking about Dylan.

She'd tossed and turned most of the night, kept awake not only by her guilt, but by remembering the touch of his lips against her own, the feel of his muscled body as he'd held her in his arms. The hard glint of passion in his eyes as he'd looked at her. Even when she'd finally drifted to sleep, her dreams had been filled with images of him kissing her, sweeping her up into his arms and taking her to his bed, images of his bare skin against her own, his hands touching her, arousing. He'd gazed down at her, his body poised over her own, his expression filled with raw desire as he spread her legs with his knee. She'd reached for him, wanting him closer, wanting him inside her.

Then suddenly anger had replaced the need in his gaze, and he was standing by the window, his eyes dark with fury as he pointed outside to where a man in a black shroud stood by a gallows.

She'd awakened then, gasping, her heart pounding wildly. Was it an omen? she'd wondered. Was she destined for failure?

There'd been no sleep for her after that, and still the awful dread, the fear, of her dream lingered.

A knock at the door made her jump, but before she could even get off the bed, Sally darted out of the dressing room and headed across the room.

Princess Megan had sent word the previous evening that she would be delighted to take Emily on a tour of the palace, and that she would arrive at Emily's room at ten o'clock. Emily had been a nervous wreck all morning, and though she'd wanted to feign a headache, she'd decided against it. Not only had Dr. Waltham approved of an outing, Emily had told enough lies already. Besides, she was clearly aware that if she was going to do as these men had demanded, then it would be important to be personally familiar with the layout of the palace.

Breath held, Emily stood and tried to ignore the flutters in her stomach. She'd already asked Sally the proper manner in which to greet a princess, and Emily prayed she didn't trip over her own feet when she curtsied.

But when Sally opened the door, it wasn't Princess Megan standing there. It was Dylan.

Sally curtsied and stepped aside. "Your Royal Highness."

Dylan nodded. "Sally."

Pulse racing, Emily hesitated, then curtsied as well. She felt terribly awkward with the whole business, but was pleased that at least she had managed to hold an upright position.

Dylan glanced at Sally. "I saw Ryan O'Connor in the garden this morning, pruning my mother's rose-bushes. He inquired about you."

Sally burst into a smile, then quickly composed herself and folded her hands primly. "Ry—Mr. O'Connor inquired about me?"

"He mentioned he hadn't seen you in a few days, and he hoped that you weren't ill."

"He thought I was ill?" The maid's eyes took on a doe-like quality, then she remembered where she was. Color rose on her cheeks. "I—I've been busy with Miss Emily."

"He seemed terribly concerned," Dylan said evenly. "Perhaps you should go set his mind at ease."

"Now?" Sally looked confused that the prince would suggest such a thing, yet hopeful just the same. "But I really shouldn't. My duties are here, in the palace, with Miss Emily and I couldn't—"

"If anyone asks—" Dylan shrugged "—tell them to see me."

Even if she'd wanted to argue with Dylan—which she didn't—Sally knew better than to deny a royal command. Excitement lit her eyes as she curtsied quickly. "Yes, Your Royal Highness."

"Was Your Highness matchmaking?" Emily asked in amazement after the maid darted out of the room.

"Certainly not." Dylan sniffed at such a ridiculous idea. "If Ryan can't concentrate on his work, my mother's rosebushes will be ruined and then there will be hell to pay." He closed the door behind him, let his gaze roam slowly down her body. "And we *are* alone now, Emily. I'm simply Dylan, remember?"

The intensity in his eyes, the suggestive tone of his voice, sent a shiver of electricity up Emily's spine. There was nothing simple at all about this man, she thought, and she certainly didn't need him to tell her that they were without a chaperon.

He'd dressed in casual clothes today, she noted. A navy tweed sports jacket over a pale-blue crew-neck sweater and tan slacks. With his dark hair and rugged looks, he radiated masculinity. And sex, she thought. How could a woman look at Dylan and not think about rumpled sheets, long hot kisses and urgent midnight whispers?

With every moment that passed, the tension stretched tighter, the air grew heavier, the room grew smaller.

"I—I was expecting Princess Megan," Emily said at last. "She sent word last night she'd be here at ten o'clock."

"She sends her apologies and regards." Dylan closed the distance between them. "She's seven months pregnant and it seems that her unborn baby kept her awake all night playing a one-man game of rugby.''

Emily winced at the thought of it, yet wondered what it would feel like to have a child growing inside her. I might never know, she realized with an ache in her chest. If she were found out, she might go to prison for the rest of her life.

''I'm so sorry,'' she said, struggled to keep her mind on Dylan instead of the possible consequences of her deceit. ''Will she be all right?''

''Just a little sore in the ribs. The doctor examined her and assured her that she and the baby are fine.''

''Good news for everyone, I'm sure.'' When his gaze strayed to her mouth, Emily felt her pulse leap.

''Very good news.''

With him standing so close, she could barely breathe, let alone think coherently. She might have taken a step back, but would have ended up touching the bed. Not a good place to be with Dylan looking at her as if he wanted nothing more than to muss up the neatly made covers and drag her between the sheets.

When he reached out and cupped her jaw in his hand, then studied her face, she sucked in a breath.

''Does it still hurt?'' His thumb moved upward and swept lightly over the bruise under her eye.

''No.'' She managed to find her voice, but kept her head still and slowly released the breath she'd been holding. Every nerve in her body had gone on alert, waiting, anticipating...

''The swelling's gone down completely,'' he observed. ''The bruise isn't nearly as dark.''

"Ice."

His gaze lifted from her cheek to her eyes. "Ice?"

"About thirty pounds, I believe. I'm surprised I haven't frostbite on my face."

He smiled, then slowly shook his head. "Your skin is warm, Emily. And soft."

So were her insides, she thought. His closeness, his touch, the deep timbre of his voice and the intensity of his gaze were making her bones melt. "Thank you," she said breathlessly.

It seemed as if the deep blue of his eyes turned darker still. His thumb traced the line of her jaw. "Shall we?" he murmured.

Her heart skipped a beat, then began to race. Isn't this why she'd come here? To be close to Dylan, to gain his confidence by whatever means necessary?

Shall we?

A simple request, not a command. His voice, his touch, seduced her. Made her want, when she had no right to want. Made her tremble with need when she required desperately to keep her composure.

Is this why he'd sent Sally off, why'd he'd wanted them to be alone?

"I—" Her voice cracked, and she swallowed. "Here?"

He lifted his head, stared at her with a mixture of amusement and desire. "Well, normally we begin the palace tours in the reception hall and ballroom, but if you'd like to start here…"

His gaze drifted to her bed.

He was talking about a tour! Emily realized, not

asking her to go to bed with him. In spite of her relief, her cheeks flamed in embarrassment.

"You—" She cleared her throat. "*You're* taking me on a tour of the palace?"

"That's what I had intended." He lowered his voice. "But if there's something else you'd rather do."

"No!" she said much too quickly, then caught herself. "I mean, I'd love to have you do it."

He lifted his brow.

"Be my guide," she added, felt her embarrassment sweep down her face and neck in a burning wave. "But you're so busy, how can you have time for such trivial things? You have meetings and appointments and—and prince things to do."

"There are no meetings scheduled until my brother returns from Drogheda, I have no appointments until late this afternoon, and I've already done my morning prince things."

He was teasing her, she knew, but still, she couldn't believe he was actually offering to be her guide.

"If you aren't up to a tour—" He tucked several loose strands of her hair behind her ear "—we could stay in."

We could stay in, he'd said. Not *you*. We.

She knew she needed to get out of here now, out of this room, away from this bed. She needed to put some distance between them so she could think. If they were in public, where other people would see them, he wouldn't touch her the way he did in private, he wouldn't look at her as though he wanted to devour her.

And if they were in public, she wouldn't want so badly for him to do all the wonderful, exciting things his touch and his eyes promised.

"Stay in?" He slid his fingertip down the side of her neck. "Or go out?"

She swayed toward him, then quickly straightened and stepped away. "I'll get my sweater."

It had been a long time since Dylan had seen his home through another's eyes. He felt pride as well as pleasure watching Emily take in the sights of Penwyck Palace. He'd started at the rear of the palace, taken her through the portrait hall, which held a gallery of ancestral paintings, the games room and theater, the back offices and the family's private quarters, then up to the front of the palace. Amazement sparkled more brightly in her green eyes with each new turn, and now, as they stood on the balcony overlooking the two-story, enormous ballroom and reception area, she'd actually gasped.

Because he'd grown up here, the opulence, the elegance of his home were normal to him, even though Dylan certainly understood that the palace was anything but "normal."

His childhood had been sheltered—private tutors, nannies, chauffeurs. And the worse of it all—bodyguards. He'd truly hated being followed and observed nearly every second of the day, had constantly devised schemes to elude their ever-watchful eyes.

On more than one occasion, he'd given his mother royal fits over his disregard for rules and his lack of discipline. And as far as his schooling—they'd practically had to tie him down to make him study.

Still, much to his teachers' and his mother's dismay, he'd breezed through math and history and physics, had finished his high-school studies by the time he was sixteen, then had gained a degree in business and English from Oxford University by the time he was twenty. After another two years as liaison to his father's European business interests, Dylan had rebelled once again. King Morgan had been furious when Dylan had informed him he was stepping down from the position. At twenty-two, there was too much to see, too much to do. Everything in his life had always been too structured, too safe. He wanted—needed—danger.

Working with Graystroke had given him that and more. For the first time in his life, he'd not only gained anonymity by changing his appearance and creating an identity for himself, he'd had true freedom.

And now that he'd experienced that freedom, now that he'd been in countries where that freedom didn't exist, he understood how precious it was. Understood the importance of being a part of his own country's government, understood that it was not just a duty, but an honor to serve the people of Penwyck.

"Dylan, it's so beautiful." Emily's voice was reverent and soft as she stared down at the ballroom. "And the staircases, they're exquisite."

He'd been standing beside her, his hands clasped

behind his back. He leaned in close and glanced down at the two grand staircases leading from the balcony area to the reception hall below. "My brother Owen and I used to slide down the banisters when we were children. Gave our nannies heart attacks."

Eyes wide with surprise, she shot him a glance over her shoulder. "So you were normal children then?"

Strange that he'd had that same thought just a moment ago. Still, he didn't miss the teasing tone in her voice. He cocked his head and gave her a half smile. "Are you saying I'm not normal now?"

She laughed. "I'm saying that children have a way of finding mischief in spite of their parents' best efforts to prevent them from doing so."

It was the first time he'd heard her laugh, Dylan realized. He liked the sound, and the sparkle in her green eyes. "You speak as if from experience, Emily. Are you remembering anything? Something about family?"

He watched the light in her eyes disappear, then she glanced away, shaking her head.

He hadn't considered that she might have children. Pierceson had told him that the bicycle vendor had said she wasn't married, but that certainly wasn't a prerequisite for babies. Or she might have been married and was now divorced, he realized, in spite of how young she was.

"It would be horrible," she whispered. "If I had family, people who cared about me, and they didn't know if I were safe, or if I were even alive."

Her voice started to shake as she spoke. Dylan took her shoulders and turned her to face him. "We've checked with the local authorities. There's been no missing person's report. If you had family, and they knew you were missing, don't you think they'd be looking for you? Wouldn't you look for someone you cared about?"

Her gaze lifted to his. "Yes."

There was torment in her eyes, Dylan noted, and it stung him. Until they knew more and could put the pieces together, he vowed to keep her mind occupied with other things.

He lifted his head, hesitated. "Do you hear that?"

She glanced around. "Hear what?"

"The music."

Eyes narrowed, she shook her head. "I don't hear anything."

"I believe it's a waltz." He cocked his head. "Ah, of course. The "Blue Danube." May I have this dance, Miss Emily?"

When he stepped away and bowed, then offered his hand, she stared at him as if he were daft. "Dylan, you don't have to—"

"Are you refusing me?" he demanded in his most empirical voice. "His Royal Highness of Penwyck?"

She looked truly flustered, then the light in her eyes returned. "Of course I'm not refusing you, Your Royal Highness. I would be honored."

She curtsied and took his hand, then he slipped his other hand around her waist and held her at arm's length. She moved into the dance with him as if the music truly were playing, followed his steps flaw-lessly as they glided across the marble floor of the balcony.

Her waist fitted perfectly in his hand, Dylan thought. He felt the heat of her body through the cotton blouse she wore, wanted desperately to feel her bare skin against his palm. Pulling her closer than the dance required, he whispered, "Are you here with anyone who would take offense at my holding you so close, Miss Emily? A lover perhaps?"

She faltered a moment, then quickly moved back into step and lowered her eyes. "Yes, Your Royal Highness. I'm here with Count Archibald Popolakis. He will be most jealous of your attentions."

"Count Popolakis," Dylan said with disdain as he whirled Emily. "I know the scoundrel. I shall command the royal army to imprison him in the dungeon."

"Oh, thank you, Your Royal Highness," Emily said with a theatrical flair. "But I should warn you. At the stroke of midnight, I will transform into an ordinary peasant girl whose entire life has been spent washing and cooking and cleaning for her three evil stepsisters and stepmother."

"Then I shall put them in the dungeon with the count and you will be mine," Dylan affirmed. "I'm in need of a woman who cooks and cleans."

The sound of her laughter rippled through him. He couldn't remember the last time he'd let himself play like this. Maybe he never had, he realized. Once a woman knew who he was, she was too busy trying to impress him or seduce him. Either way, he'd never been bothered by a woman's ulterior motive to get close to him. If they'd ended up in bed, then it had been mutually pleasant for both of them.

Yet something was different with Emily. He knew that he wanted her in his bed, that part wasn't different. He'd spent most of the night pacing his bedroom, his body frustrated with wanting her. That part of his feelings he understood completely. What he didn't understand was the depth of his need to watch over her. To make sure she was all right. To be with her. The pleasure he felt just in making her laugh.

He frowned at the direction his thoughts had taken, then shook his head at his foolishness. Sex, he told himself. What he felt for Emily wasn't anything more than the physical attraction between a man and a woman. There was a lot happening in the palace and the country right now. He was tense, that was all.

And he knew the best way to relieve that tension.

He whirled her suddenly. She gasped at the unexpected move. Before she could speak, he pulled her close and covered her mouth with his.

Six

Every thought in Emily's mind stopped. The moment Dylan's mouth pressed against her own, it seemed to her as if the entire world had stopped. For that split second, she couldn't breathe, couldn't pull away. She knew he held her in his arms, that he was kissing her, but she simply couldn't react.

Then the floodgates opened and every emotion poured free, a rushing wave of heat and desire and despair.

If only she'd seen it coming. If she had, she might have prepared herself somehow, shielded herself from the stunning explosion of need that rocked her to the core. But he'd caught her off guard and she'd had no time, no defenses.

The breath she'd been holding shuddered loose, then she moved into him, needing his closeness with an intensity that shocked her. His mouth was insistent, but not demanding. He tipped her head back, nibbled on one corner of her mouth, then lightly swept his tongue over her bottom lip. She opened to him, moaned softly when he dipped inside.

It was glorious, she thought dimly. The faint taste of mint, the masculine scent of his skin, the press of his hard body against hers. She felt all the colors of a rainbow stream through her—brilliant yellow, cool blue, hot red. Felt the textures of soft velvet, smooth silk and hard steel. They all swirled together in a kaleidoscope of need.

He deepened the kiss, and she slipped her hands up his chest, felt the heavy beat of his heart under her palms. Her own heart raced, and she realized that kissing Dylan did feel very much like a race, that her own body betrayed her by wanting desperately to reach the finish line. She slid her arms upward, around his neck, rose on her tiptoes so that she might feel him closer still. His mouth slanted against hers, his tongue explored, tasted deeply.

Somewhere in the distance, she heard voices, was certain they were inside her head until Dylan broke the kiss. She swayed on weak knees, felt his hands steady her, then quickly pull her away from the balcony railing behind a pair of heavy, deep-green brocade drapes.

"It appears we weren't the only tour group today," Dylan said irritably.

The voices grew louder, and Emily realized that they were coming from the ballroom below. She peeked around the edge of the drapes and saw a large group of people gathered in the center of the reception hall. From their vantage point, the group would easily have seen her and Dylan locked in a passionate kiss on the balcony.

She started to pull back when a man in the group caught her attention. A tall man wearing a black leather jacket. Shaved head, evil eyes.

Sutton.

That horrible man had actually come here, to the palace! Gasping, she lurched back, instinctively clung to Dylan. It took every ounce of strength she possessed not to step out into the open, to point at the man and demand he be arrested.

But what good would that do? The men holding her grandmother would find out, and then they would surely—

No. She closed her eyes and willed the thought to be gone. She couldn't even think of them harming Olivia. She couldn't.

"Are you all right?"

"They almost saw us." She opened her eyes, wrapped her fingers into the front of the light sweater he wore. "They almost saw us."

"It's all right." He pressed a kiss to her temple. "It wouldn't have been the end of the world if they'd seen us. Just an annoyance."

"No...I—" She couldn't speak, couldn't tell him the truth, though she desperately wanted to.

"You're pale." Worry furrowed his brow. He covered her hands with his. "And your hands are like ice."

"I'm all right." She loosened the death grip she

had on his sweater. "I'm tired, that's all. I should go back now."

He stared at her for a long moment, then nodded. "All right. We'll do the grounds when you're feeling better."

"Thank you." She started to pull away, but he held her close to him. She lifted her gaze, saw the resolve in his eyes.

"The next time I kiss you," he said firmly, "I'll be certain there are no interruptions."

Her heart slammed against her ribs, but she said nothing. The sound of voices grew louder as the tour group began to move up the stairs. Panic shivered up her spine. She knew if she saw Sutton, if they made eye contact, she might jeopardize everything.

"We should go," she said.

He released her then, touched the small of her back and guided her down the corridor in the direction from which they'd come.

They were both quiet on the walk back. Emily's insides were wound into tight little knots. And though her body still hummed from Dylan's kiss, knowing that Sutton was in the palace set her already frayed nerves on edge.

By the time they reached the door to her quarters, Emily felt she might quite literally shatter if Dylan touched her. She needed space from him right now. At least a continent, she thought, but knew that even then she'd think about him. That she'd hate herself for what she'd done, but she'd want him just the same.

"Thank you for the tour, Dylan." She reached for

the doorknob, prayed he wouldn't see her hand was shaking. "The palace is beautiful, and I appreciate the time you've taken from your busy schedule to show me around."

"A pleasure, my lady." A smile lifted the corners of his mouth when he leaned forward, then lifted his hand to trace the line of her jaw with his fingertip. "Though I hope the pleasure was not mine alone."

Just a touch, a simple brush of his finger on her skin, sent ripples of heat through her blood. Afraid she might embarrass herself, that she might lean into that touch and ask for more, she dropped her gaze. It was much easier to stare at Dylan's shoes. If she looked into his eyes, she'd be lost for certain.

"As much as I would have enjoyed a quiet evening alone with you—" his finger slid back up to the lobe of her ear, then he sighed and dropped his arm away "—I regret I have previous plans this evening."

Another woman? she wondered, then realized how ridiculous the thought was. What did it matter what it was he was busy doing? She knew it was dangerous and extremely foolish to let herself feel anything for Dylan. There could never be anything between them. She'd made certain of that from the first lie she'd told.

She looked up at him, prayed he couldn't see through the mask of nonchalance she struggled to project. "You've been more than generous with your time."

"I have a conference call with my brother in the morning and a business lunch with the Duke of Sydebottom tomorrow. I will pick you up after that and we'll finish the tour.''

It wasn't a request, Emily realized, but more like a royal decree. ''Finish the tour?''

''You haven't seen the palace grounds. The weather is supposed to be nice tomorrow,'' he said. ''We'll walk through the gardens.''

She wanted to protest, to insist it wasn't necessary for him to take her on a tour, but based on the set look on his face and the resolve in his eyes, she was certain her objection would go unheeded.

''That would be lovely.'' She felt a mixture of dread and excitement of being outside alone with Dylan, away from the palace and its staff. ''Thank you again for a lovely afternoon.''

She slipped into her room, leaving him out in the hallway, then closed her eyes and leaned back against the door. Pressing her fingers to her mouth, she tried not to remember the feel of Dylan's lips on hers and the betrayal not only of her own body when she'd responded so eagerly to his kiss, but the betrayal that had brought her here in the first place.

She hadn't much time, she knew.

Tonight, while Dylan was out, she would break into his suite.

Briefcase in hand, Dylan armed the alarm panel to his suite, closed the door behind him, then headed for the elevator at the end of the hall where he punched in another set of numbers at the elevator keypad and stepped inside. He glanced briefly at the camera over his head, knew that his image was already on the security monitors. The temptation to make a rude gesture always overcame him when he stepped into the elevator, but he managed to resist. A man with a mission as serious as his should never draw attention to himself, he knew only too well.

The elevator shuddered to a stop at the basement level. Dylan stepped off and nodded to the guard posted there, then made his way through a private tunnel underneath the palace. At the first fork he turned left and passed the offices where Penwyck's Royal Elite Team was headquartered. Several guards in this area straightened and greeted him as he passed, but he didn't pause, afraid if he stopped, they might suspect what he was up to. If he were caught with the contraband in his briefcase, there would be serious consequences.

At the end of the tunnel, Dylan climbed a set of stairs to a pair of doors, where two guards immediately stood tall. A sign over the door in red letters read, Authorized Personnel Only.

''Your Royal Highness,'' the men said together, then opened the doors for Dylan. He nodded as he passed through and entered a small lobby. To one side of the room, three tapestry armchairs faced a chocolate-brown velvet couch. On the other side was the private nurse's station reserved for the members of the royal family.

''Good evening, Your Royal Highness,'' the nurse greeted him from behind the counter.

''Evening, Jennifer.'' Dylan's hand tightened around the handle of his briefcase, but he kept his tone light as he made his way across the room. "Dora off tonight?"

"Yes, Your Highness." Jennifer smiled. "Home with the family."

He moved through another door, which led to a wing of rooms, then knocked lightly on the first door to the left. A secret service agent named Jack Myers opened the door, greeted Dylan, then stepped aside to allow him entry.

King Morgan, dressed in a long, deep-blue robe and slippers, rose from a plush chair where he'd been reading his evening paper. Dylan still found it difficult to believe that a man as robust as his father had been as ill as he had, especially since he'd been recovering so quickly these past few days.

"Well, it's about damn time."

"Good evening, Father."

Morgan dragged a hand through his short, wavy brown hair and frowned at his son, then shot a glance at Myers. "Leave us."

"But, Your Majesty, the queen has—"

"I said, *leave us!*" King Morgan roared. "As long as I'm still breathing, I'm the king."

Obviously nervous, the man glanced from Morgan to Dylan, then bowed and reluctantly left the room.

"We haven't much time." Morgan moved to a desk and sat in the chair. "Your mother has spies everywhere. Do you have it?"

Dylan stepped beside his father, laid the briefcase on the desk, opened it then pulled out a plastic case and handed it to his father.

King Morgan opened the case and stared at the

corned beef on rye sandwich. Pleasure brightened his face as he picked the sandwich up and took a bite. Closing his eyes, he groaned with delight. "What I wouldn't give for an ale to go with this."

"Absolutely not." Dylan settled into the leather armchair across from his father. "Mother will have both our heads if she finds out about this, and Dr. Waltham will banish me from the infirmary all together."

"Oatmeal, poached eggs and boiled chicken. They feed the royal horses and pigs better than their own king," Morgan grumbled around another bite, then, overcome with rapture, sank back in his chair. "Now tell me what's going on outside this dungeon I've been exiled to."

Morgan listened thoughtfully while Dylan brought him up to date with the palace business. Owen was currently in Drogheda, negotiating an alliance with the neighboring island and the island of Marjorco, as well; two known members of the Black Knights had been spotted at a pub in town, but they'd escaped before they could be apprehended; Broderick, Morgan's brother, had been forced to step down as the temporary ruler of Penwyck, and there was suspicion that Broderick himself was linked to the group of rebel dissidents.

"Damn the traitorous bastard." Morgan shook his head in disgust. "To think my own flesh and blood would jeopardize this country and his own family members infuriates me. Have we proof?"

"Not yet." Dylan put the plastic sandwich case back in his briefcase and closed it. He knew it was important to remove all incriminating evidence. "The Royal Elite Team has been working on locating the Black Knights' headquarters, but so far every lead has turned into a dead end."

Morgan leaned forward and put a hand on Dylan's shoulder. "I've missed you these past two years, son. You ready to tell me what you were doing all that time?"

Dylan grinned at his father. "Chasing women and drinking myself blind every night, of course. What else?"

King Morgan gave a bellowing laugh, then turned his attention back to the last of his sandwich. "I've taught you well, my boy, though God forbid your mother hears me say that. Women haven't much of a sense of humor about these things."

Dylan didn't suppose his mother would have much of a sense of humor over the fact that her son had been working for a special forces group in Borovkia, either. Better to let his parents think he'd been carousing these past two years, rather than being part of a covert search and rescue for kidnapped businessmen and innocent civilians.

King Morgan brushed the crumbs off the front of his robe, then settled back in his chair and studied his son thoughtfully. "And speaking of women, I've been hearing some interesting stories about a certain dark-haired beauty you're infatuated with. Emma, is it?"

Dylan felt the flash of annoyance, then shook it off. He knew there were no secrets in the palace, that the entire staff most likely knew what color socks he wore on any given day. He'd had to live with lack of privacy his entire life. He could only accept it as part of who he was, who his family was.

But that still didn't mean he had to like it, either.

"Emily," he said more irritably than he'd intended. "And I'm not infatuated. I just feel a certain sense of responsibility, that's all. I nearly killed the woman, for God's sake."

"Responsibility, is it?" Morgan raised an eyebrow. "With a bit of lust thrown in to ease the bitter taste?"

In spite of his annoyance, Dylan smiled, then shrugged. "Perhaps."

Morgan grinned. "A healthy thing, lust. Enjoy yourself while you're young, son. I remember when your mother and I—" he stopped abruptly, then cleared his throat. "Well, never mind. Let's have a game of cards, shall we?"

Thankful that he wouldn't have to hear about his parents' sexual exploits in their younger days, Dylan reached for the deck of cards on the desk top and shuffled them. "Rummy?"

King Morgan snorted. "Five-card draw. I win, tomorrow you bring a cigar."

"All right." With those stakes, Dylan knew he'd have to make certain he didn't lose. "And if I win, you have to eat your poached eggs and boiled chicken until Dr. Waltham says different."

"Dr. Waltham is a buffoon," Morgan complained, then rubbed his hands together briskly. "Deal the cards, son."

* * *

Bright silver streaks of moonlight poured through the windows and streamed across the plush carpeted floors. Emily lay in bed, staring at her closed bedroom door, listening for any sounds from the hallway outside. Other than the fierce pounding of her own heart, the palace was exceptionally quiet tonight.

Sally had been a wealth of information regarding the royal family's plans this evening. Without even asking, Emily had learned that the queen and her daughters were entertaining the Duke and Duchess of Haberson, that Prince Owen was away, and Prince Dylan had given his valet the evening off, which usually meant, Sally had said with a sparkle in her eyes, that His Royal Highness would be dining elsewhere and not returning until the morning.

Emily knew that she should be elated over the news. Wasn't this exactly what she needed—for Dylan to be away for the evening? How else was she going to sneak inside his suite without his knowing?

But she wasn't elated at all. She was terrified. She was certain she would be caught, that she'd be arrested, then taken away in handcuffs while everyone who'd been so nice to her looked on in shock and disgust.

She squeezed her eyes shut and fisted the sheets in her hands. She couldn't think about that, she couldn't. She had to think success, had to think about her grandmother being safely released and nothing else.

And though she'd tried to deny it all afternoon, there was something else she had to admit, as well: she hated the idea of Dylan with another woman,

especially after the way he'd kissed her this afternoon.

Did he kiss every woman the way he'd kissed her?
she wondered. Did he make every woman feel as if
her bones might melt, as if no other man had existed
before? As if no other man ever would?

Of course he did, she'd told herself a hundred
times since she'd returned to her room. She knew
that he wanted her, physically wanted her—he'd certainly made that clear. But that didn't mean there
was anything at all special about her, the way a
woman wants to be special to a man.

She'd waited her entire life to find a man who
would make her feel this way—as if there were but-
terflies in her stomach. As if her feet were barely
touching the ground. As if colors were brighter and
sounds were sharper.

She sighed at her foolishness, then slid out from
under the covers. She shivered at the cool air and
pulled a robe on over the green satin pajamas she
wore. It was only nine-thirty; she'd give herself fifteen minutes tops, then be back in this room. Tucking her feet into the soft forest-green slippers beside
her bed, she made her way across the room. Quietly,
she opened her door and peered out into the hall.

It was empty.

Dylan's quarters were around the corner from her
own. He'd pointed out his suite to her when he'd
taken her on the tour this morning, had made it clear
that he was close if she needed anything. Anything
at all.

But she'd already known where Dylan's quarters

were. Sutton had given her a map of the palace and insisted she commit it to memory before she destroyed it, along with the entry code that would gain her access into Dylan's suite and the combination of the safe inside.

A moment later, as she stood in front of the softly lit security panel, her legs shook.

She knew the code. All she had to do was enter the numbers, then slip inside. It should be easy. She only needed a few minutes to get in and get out. There were no security cameras here, she'd been told. The royal family insisted on privacy in their quarters.

A privacy she was about to intrude on.

If only there was another way.

The truth? she wondered. Would Dylan help her if she told him the truth? Or would he have her thrown in jail, leaving Olivia in the hands of those horrible men?

She couldn't risk that. She had no other choice but to proceed with the plan.

She glanced around the empty hallway, then closed her eyes and drew in a slow, calming breath. *I can do this. I can.* Heart pounding, palms sweating, she lifted her hand to the control panel.

"Emily?"

She whirled at the sound of Dylan's voice at the end of the hall. He stood there, briefcase in his hand, a dark frown on his face.

She couldn't speak. Couldn't move. Couldn't breathe.

His frown darkened as he walked toward her. "What are you doing here?"

Seven

"Is something wrong?" Dylan asked impatiently when she didn't answer him. He'd been so lost in his thoughts, thoughts of her, wondering if she were sleeping, what she would look like with that amazing hair of hers spread across her pillow—across *his* pillow. How much he wanted to wrap his hands in that hair and pull her to him, underneath him.

And then he found her, standing at his door, as if he'd conjured her up just by thinking of her.

Wearing her nightclothes, no less.

When she still didn't answer him, he pushed the buttons on his alarm panel, then took hold of her arm and quickly pulled her inside his suite. Though most of the palace staff was gone by this hour, there was always an occasional maid or valet wandering the hallways. Obviously, there were enough rumors flying about the palace, he didn't need to add any more fuel to that fire.

It was dark inside. He could have reached for the light switch, but he set his briefcase down on the marble floor of the foyer and reached for Emily instead.

"Are you ill?" He slid his hands up to her shoulders. "Shall I call for the doctor?"

"No, no, I'm fine. You just startled me."

"You're trembling."

"I—I had a dream," she said. "It was so real. I know it's silly of me. I certainly shouldn't be bothering you, but—"

"You're not bothering me." He pulled her into his arms, smoothed his hand up her stiff spine, then down again. When she started to push away, he held her firmly against him. "Relax, Emily. I won't bite," he said softly. "Unless you ask me to, of course."

Still shivering, she pressed her cheek against his shirt. He breathed in her faint floral scent, felt the heat of her skin, the rapid pounding of her heart. His body tightened in response, but he held back from pulling her closer still, from tugging open the belt of her robe and dipping his hands inside to fill his palms with the soft, firm weight of her breasts.

But he was only human. He knew his limits, knew he couldn't take much more of this and not give in to the demands of his body.

He stepped away, took her arm and led her to the sofa in his parlor. A river of moonlight through the windows cast a silvery edge to the shadows. "Sit here. I'll be right back."

He crossed to the buffet table where his valet kept a full-service bar stocked, dropped ice into two crystal glasses, then poured Scotch into each one.

She hesitated when he pressed the glass into her hand, then she took a sip. When she started to cough, he smiled and sat down beside her.

"Well, I suppose that tells us you don't drink much," he said. "The next sip should go down easier, though. Now tell me about your dream."

She took another sip, closed her eyes as she swallowed, then opened them again. "I'm in a room. There's a window with bars and a man reaches in to grab me. Every corner I run to, he's there, his fingers clutching and clawing at me. I can't get away from him."

Dylan couldn't see Emily's face clearly, but her voice shook with fear. He took the glass from her hands and set it on the side table, then set his down, as well.

"Do you know this man?" He pulled her close, amazed at his need to comfort. "Does he have a face?"

"No." Her fingers curled into the front of his shirt. He couldn't see her eyes, but he could feel her gaze, intense and frightened. "But he's real, Dylan. He does exist."

Did he? Dylan wondered. Or was it just a dream? A nightmare she couldn't quite let go?

"No one's going to hurt you." He smoothed her

hair back from her shoulders. "I won't let anyone hurt you."

She loosened her hold on his shirt, then, with a sigh, she slid her hand up his chest and laid her palm on his cheek. "Thank you."

The gentle touch of her fingertips on his face made his blood heat. He turned his mouth into her hand, pressed his lips to her palm. "Come to my bed, Emily. Stay with me."

He felt her hesitation, then her shudder. He moved his lips to her wrist and nibbled there, tasted the warmth of her skin, felt the rapid-fire beat of her pulse.

"You don't even know who I am," she whispered.

"I want you," he said firmly. "You want me, I know you do. That's enough for now."

"For now, maybe." Her hand slid away from his face. "But what about tomorrow, or the day after that?"

"There's only now," he insisted, felt the need pumping through his body. "Just you and me."

"If only that were true." She eased away from him, pulled her robe tightly around her. "I—I'm sorry. But I can't. I just can't."

She stood, then hurried from the room. He started to go after her, then stopped. He'd certainly never forced a woman into going to bed with him before, and he had no intention of starting now, even though his body screamed different.

Dammit! He couldn't remember when any woman had frustrated him so completely.

Though he didn't like it, he supposed he could understand why she'd be reluctant to make love with him if she didn't know who she was. There was the possibility that she had a lover, a boyfriend, even a fiancé, though she wore no ring.

He narrowed his eyes at the thought. He didn't give a damn if there was another man in her life—unless she was married, of course. That was one line he would never cross. But he did not believe she was married. As far as he was concerned, Emily belonged to him.

He picked up his glass of Scotch and drained it. He'd never been a patient man, but he'd give her more time if she needed it.

With a sigh, he laid his head back on the sofa and hoped to God she didn't make him wait long.

The next afternoon, as he'd promised, Dylan arrived at Emily's room to take her on a tour of the palace grounds. She'd been anxious and tense all morning while she'd waited for the prince, but now that they'd been strolling in the warm, fresh air for the past hour, she found herself finally starting to relax and even enjoy the opportunity to be away from the confines of her room.

The palace outside was every bit as beautiful as it was inside. Sparkling marble fountains, formal gardens, a towering white gazebo and tennis court. And though it was winter and the roses had been pruned down to the barest stubs, Emily could picture the bushes in full bloom come spring. Bright pinks, soft yellows, deep reds. Lavenders, whites and every

shade of orange. She could even imagine how sweet
the air would smell, filled with the exotic scents of
thousands of flowers.

She'd never see or smell them, she knew, but she
let herself dream for a moment as she walked along
a rock path beside Dylan. He'd been explaining how
the marble used in the fountains and the interior floors
of the palace was mined in the Aronleigh Mountains
and brought by trucks to local tradesmen to be finished.

He'd dressed casually again today, tan slacks, a
white polo shirt and dark-brown boots. Emily was
thankful that Sally had laid out the comfortable
clothes she had on—black slacks, a pale pink, long-
sleeved cotton blouse and soft leather walking shoes,
though she was certain it had not been coincidental.
From the first night Emily had been brought here,
Dylan had seen to her comfort, had paid attention to
every detail, made sure that she had everything she
could possibly want or need. He'd been wonderful to
her, had made her feel special.

Like a princess.

She watched him as he pointed out one of the garden statues, commenting that it was fashioned after
the Minotaur, the mythic creature who was half-bull,
half-human and every nine years feasted on seven
maidens and seven youths. He spoke of the Labyrinth,
where the creature had been contained, how its hap-
less victims were released into the twisting, endless
maze, and then devoured by the beast.

Emily was certain she knew how those poor people
must have felt. Wandering about a maze with no

escape, knowing they were about to be devoured. A feeling of utter hopelessness.

He'd nearly caught her last night.

Every time she thought of it, she had to remind herself to breathe. Ten seconds more, less than that, and he would have seen her pushing the buttons on his alarm. Or if she'd managed to get inside his suite—Dear God!—he would have found her there. He would have known, would have seen her for the liar she was.

And still, in spite of everything, she'd nearly gone to his bed last night. She'd wanted to, had wanted to be in the safety of his arms, had wanted to forget about everything else, if only for a little while.

If she hadn't been such a coward, if she'd been thinking about her grandmother instead of herself, she would have gone to bed with Dylan. She could have waited for the right moment, when he was deeply asleep, or maybe in the shower, and opened the safe behind the Monet oil painting in his study. She would have found the information they'd demanded of her, and this nightmare would be over.

Or would it? she wondered. Would it ever truly be over, whatever the outcome?

"Hello, Emily," Dylan whispered in her ear, making her jump. "Where are you?"

Her cheeks flushed as she realized he'd caught her not paying attention. "I—I'm sorry. I'm a little lost in all the beauty here. Forgive me."

Smiling, he took her hand and kissed her fingers. Electricity sizzled up her arm and raced through her body.

"I find myself a little lost, as well," he said, keeping his eyes on her face. "And I'll forgive you if you tell me you were thinking about me."

This, she thought, was a question she could answer truthfully. She met his intense gaze. "I was."

His hand tightened on hers, and he bent toward her, his eyes on her mouth now. Her pulse skipped as she lifted her face, felt her lashes flutter down as he drew closer—

The quiet sound of someone clearing their throat made Emily jerk away. Frowning, Dylan stepped back.

A pretty young woman stood a few feet away, watching Dylan with obvious interest. Shiny light-brown hair streaked with blond tumbled around the shoulders of her cotton blouse and a calf-length beige skirt hugged her slender hips and covered the tops of her low-heeled black boots.

"Hello, Dylan," the woman said, then glanced at Emily and smiled. "You must be the mysterious Emily.'

"Emily." Dylan swept a hand toward the other woman. "May I introduce my sister, Princess Anastasia."

One look at the woman's eyes would have told Emily that this woman was related to Dylan. They were the same striking blue. Emily curtsied. "Your Royal Highness."

Princess Anastasia smiled. "I'm glad to see you're feeling better. I heard my brother plowed you down with his limo when you were out bicycling."

"It was my fault completely," Emily said awkwardly. "I shouldn't have been in the road, and he couldn't have—"

"Ignore my sister," Dylan said dryly. "She has an odd sense of humor at times."

"But you love me, anyway." Anastasia moved forward to give her brother a peck on the cheek. "I wouldn't miss an opportunity to take a dig at you, would I?"

"Nor I, you," he returned and grinned. "I was just showing Emily the Minotaur."

"Is that what you were doing?" she said with a twinkle in her eyes, then glanced at Emily. "Did my brother tell you that my sisters and I renamed this statue Dylan? You know, half-bull, half-man."

Emily smiled, though it was clear that Dylan did not see the humor in Anastasia's revelation regarding the statue.

"I thought you had a fund-raiser at the hospital today," Dylan said with a sigh.

Anastasia glanced at the gold watch on her wrist. "And so I do. I've got you down for a hefty donation to the children's ward, Dylan. I'll stop by later for a check."

He nodded, then Anastasia turned to Emily and offered a hand. "A pleasure to meet you, Emily."

Emily took the princess's hand, couldn't help but feel the warmth and sincerity Anastasia radiated. "The pleasure was mine."

Anastasia gave her brother another kiss on the cheek. "Forgive me for intruding on your—" she hesitated and smiled "—tour."

She walked away then, leaving Dylan to frown after her.

"A man with three sisters has no childhood secrets," he complained. "And even less privacy."

He took Emily's hand suddenly, pulled her along the rock path behind him. She could barely keep up with his long strides as he led her off the path onto a graveled driveway leading to the building where the palace vehicles were garaged and maintained.

"Dylan, what are you—"

He pressed a finger to his lips to quiet her, then glanced around the garage. There were three shiny black limousines, two Town Cars, three compacts, and a sleek forest-green Jaguar. Emily heard the muffled voices of men talking from an office in the back of the garage, and a radio sitting on a work bench poured out a Celtic tune about highway robbers.

Dylan opened the passenger door of the Jaguar, nodded for her to get inside. She sank into the soft seat, and the smell of leather and freshly polished wood filled her senses.

"What are you doing?" she asked when Dylan slipped into the driver's seat and started the car.

"We're playing hooky for the afternoon." He grinned at her, then turned the key in the ignition.

The engine purred so silently she wasn't certain it was even running. Emily thought of her own twenty-year-old Fiat that choked and gasped every time she started it. And though she'd seen Jaguars and other fancy cars when she'd gone to university in Wales, she'd never ridden in such a fine, elegant car as this one. Her breath caught when Dylan turned and brushed his shoulder against hers, then reached across her. For one heart-stopping moment, she thought he was going to kiss her, felt her skin heat up, then tighten at the close contact. But he didn't kiss her. Instead, he grabbed the seat belt, then snapped it into place.

By the time she managed to release the breath she'd been holding, they were heading up a private mountain road to the west of the palace.

She glanced over at Dylan. "Where are we going?"

"There's something I want to show you." He opened the sun roof, let the fresh air and the warm sun inside the car. "Did you have any more dreams last night?"

About you, she could have said. What little sleep she'd managed to get had been filled with images of Dylan, erotic dreams where he'd kissed and touched her, until she held out her arms to him and begged him to make love to her. He'd stripped her naked, then abruptly, the passion that had been in his eyes had died, replaced by cold anger as he'd seen her for what she really was.

She certainly couldn't tell him about *that* dream.

"No," she lied, kept her gaze outside the window to the passing pine trees and jutting rocks. The Jaguar hugged the road, smoothly took the next hairpin turn and continued to climb upward.

"Won't your family worry if you disappear like this?" she asked. "You didn't tell anyone where you were going."

"They'll find me if they need to."

He offered no more than that, and she didn't press. She was happy to be away from the palace, if only for a little while. She'd always loved the mountains, had gone camping and fishing with her father and grandfather when she was a little girl.

The road narrowed and grew steeper, the forest around them thickened. When they crossed over a wooden bridge, Emily heard the sound of rushing water underneath.

He pulled the car under a stand of trees, then cut the engine. "Close your eyes."

"What?"

"Close your eyes."

She did as he asked, heard him open his door, then shut it. A moment later he opened her door and had her hand in his, pulling her out of her seat.

"Keep your eyes closed," he insisted.

Pine needles crunched under her shoes as he led her away from the car. Birds chirped noisily overhead. They walked quite a distance, and twice, when she stumbled, he steadied her, but still insisted she keep her eyes tightly shut.

"Okay, stop."

He put his hands on her arms, then moved behind her. She felt the breeze on her face, caught the scent of salt water, heard the wild crash of waves.

"Open."

She did, and gasped.

They stood on the edge of a high cliff. Deep-blue ocean stretched as far as the eye could see, rushed in to pound the beach below, then rushed out again, spraying foam and water amongst the jagged rocks. Overhead, seagulls soared, screeched at the sight of intruders, then dive-bombed into the ocean in search of a snack.

"Oh, Dylan," she breathed. "It's so beautiful."

"I was hoping you'd like it."

She heard the pleasure in his voice, felt it shimmer

from his body into her own. His arms circled her waist and pulled her closer. She let herself lean against his strength.

"How could I not?" She felt lighter than she had in days. Her heart, her spirit seemed to soar with the gulls overhead. Being surrounded by this beauty filled her with a sense of supreme magnificence. A sense of hope, and a strange sense that everything wrong would somehow be made right.

In spite of the sun, the air was crisp and the icy breeze made her shiver. Dylan's arms tightened around her and she shivered again, though this time not from the breeze.

"You're cold," he murmured, then stepped away. "Come with me."

She turned, was about to protest until she spotted the small, vine-covered brick cottage no more than twenty yards away. It sat on the edge of the cliff, nestled amongst a few small pines, staring out over the ocean, like a woman waiting for her lover to return home.

Dylan took her hand, led her over the rough rock path. He opened the unlocked door and pulled her inside. The room was masculine, dark woods, heavy beams across a vaulted ceiling, stone fireplace and hardwood floors. Floor-to-ceiling windows overlooked the ocean.

She couldn't imagine anything more perfect, more inviting. Still, she hesitated at the door, glanced at him curiously.

"It's mine," he answered her unspoken question. "A gift on my eighteenth birthday."

He closed the door behind them and moved to the fireplace.

She would have known it was his even if he hadn't told her. She could feel him here, his energy, his essence. There were rows of books on a built-in pine shelf beside the fireplace, a sturdy beige sofa and two dark-brown plaid armchairs, a family picture in a silver frame on a small corner desk.

She watched as he struck a match and held it to a readied stack of firewood and kindling inside the fireplace. The kindling caught quickly and a small flame flickered, then rose.

"The kitchen is through there," he said, pointing to a door beside the bookshelf. "I keep the pantry stocked, and there's cheese and a few edibles in the refrigerator if you're hungry."

"Thank you. I'm fine." Captivated, she moved to the windows, hugged her arms as she glanced out at the endless ocean. She felt as if they were hundreds, thousands of miles from the rest of the world.

"The room will warm up in a few minutes." He stepped behind her, rubbed her arms briskly. "So what do you think?"

That was the problem. She couldn't think. Didn't want to think. He was too close, and his hands on her arms had slowed and moved upward to her shoulders.

"It's wonderful," she said, heard the breathless quality of her own voice.

"Relax, Emily. You've knots in your neck that would make a sailor proud."

His hands, those amazing, incredible hands, worked on those knots. She closed her eyes, bit her lip to keep herself from moaning with pleasure. He soothed the tension in her neck and shoulders, but created a new and different tension in her body.

She felt as if she'd become part of her surroundings: the flames from the fireplace snapped inside her, the distant pounding of the surf pulsed through her veins. She leaned back against the hard wall of Dylan's chest, let herself melt into him.

Tell him, a small voice whispered in her ear. *Tell him the truth. You can trust him, he'll help you.*

She tried to concentrate on that voice, told herself to listen, but when he lowered his head and touched his lips to the side of her neck, every thought flew out of her head. When he nipped at her earlobe, she moaned.

He turned her to face him, slid his arms around her and brought his mouth within a whisper of her own. "I want you, Emily. Let me love you."

His words, spoken with such need, such intensity, were her undoing. She could deny him no longer. Could deny herself no longer. She wrapped her arms around his neck, afraid she might fall if she didn't hold on.

"Yes," she murmured, and rose on her tiptoes. "Yes."

Eight

Mine, Dylan thought as he covered Emily's mouth with his own. His heart slammed in his chest, and when her tongue met his, a shy tentative touch, he reined in his need to take her quickly, roughly. Don't frighten her, he told himself. It might kill him, but he would take this slowly, take *her* slowly.

Through a will of iron, he kept the kiss gentle, nipped at the corner of her mouth, nibbled at her bottom lip before he dipped back in again. She opened eagerly, her breath quickening with every thrust, every hot, wet slide of his tongue against hers.

He moved his hands up her back, her neck, then dug his fingers into her thick, glossy hair. He tilted her head back, tasted more deeply. She made a sound, a soft whimper; he lifted his head, gazed down at her. Her cheeks were flushed, her lips swollen and wet from his kiss.

Her lashes fluttered open, and he saw the need shimmer in her smoky-green eyes. "Tell me you want me," he demanded. He needed to hear her say it, needed to know she had no doubts.

"I want you, Dylan." Her lips parted, waiting, ready. "I do want you."

He ground his mouth against hers again, relieved there'd been no hesitation in her reply. The ache he'd felt turned into a living, breathing beast inside him, pounded in his veins as fiercely as the surf pounded the rocks below them.

She gasped when he suddenly swept her into his arms to carry her to his bedroom. To his bed.

You belong to me, was his thought as he pushed the bedroom door open with his boot and moved inside. He held her tightly, possessively, kissed her again, and with his mouth still on hers, let her slide intimately down the length of his body.

Emily spread her hands on Dylan's chest, felt the ripple of hard muscle under her fingers and the fast, heavy thud of his heart. She'd spoken the truth a moment ago. She *did* want him, with a desperation that stunned her. But in spite of the need racing through her blood, guilt crept along the edges of what little rational thought she had left.

She had to tell him the truth. She didn't care what happened to her, only her grandmother. Surely he would help. Dylan was a good person, he wouldn't let any harm come to an old woman.

You can trust him, she told herself. She *had* to trust him.

She struggled to pull her thoughts together, to find the words she needed, but his kisses were insistent, and his hands moving over her confused and excited her.

"Dylan, wait—" she dragged her mouth from his. "Please, I need—"

"Tell me what you need," he murmured. "Is it this?"

She sucked in a breath when his lips moved to her neck.

"Dylan…"

"Is this what you need?" His hands slid upward and cupped her breasts. She gasped when he squeezed lightly, then found her nipples with his thumbs and circled the already hardened peaks.

She needed to tell him something, she was certain of it, but the sensations rippling through her body, wave after warm wave of pleasure, left her helpless and weak. Dizzy.

One by one, he opened the buttons on her blouse, then pressed his mouth to the shoulder he'd bared. He nipped at her naked skin with his lips and his teeth, made her tremble, then sigh.

And then her blouse was gone, and she stood before him in her bra. While his mouth continued to brew magic on her shoulder, his fingers slowly skimmed the rise of her breasts, then traced the edge of white lace to the front clasp. A quick flick and it popped open, then slid to the floor.

"Or perhaps this is what you need," he said huskily. He lowered his mouth to her breast and tasted.

On a soft moan, she dug her hands into his thick hair. His tongue, hot and wet and skilled, flicked her pearled nipple, laved the sensitive tip until she thought she could stand no more, then he pulled her more deeply into his mouth, tugging, sucking, in a rhythm that sent white-hot arrows of intense pleasure shooting straight to the core of her womanhood.

She'd never experienced anything like this before, had never known such passion. It frightened, yet thrilled and excited her at the same time. She felt as if she might break apart any moment, or simply die from pleasure this intense. The ache steadily growing between her legs bordered on pain.

"I need you," she gasped when he turned his attention to her other breast. "Dylan, please..."

He ignored her, continued to drive her crazy with his mouth and his hands. Her mind swirled with sensations, sights and sounds, colors. Her blood rushed hot through her veins.

When she started to tug at his shirt, he lifted his head and yanked the garment off, then pulled her into his arms again and caught her mouth to his. They stood bare torso to bare torso, warm skin against warm skin. She held on to the thick, corded muscles of his upper arms, felt the ripple of sinew under her hands, then slid her fingers up his powerful shoulders and wrapped her arms around his neck.

With his mouth still on hers, he scooped her up in his arms and laid her on the large bed, then rose over her. She trembled, part fear, part need and anticipation, and lifted her arms to him. He bent down, kissed her deeply, thoroughly, until she writhed under him, whimpering for more.

Those small sounds of need were nearly Dylan's undoing. It took every last ounce of willpower not to simply free himself from the tortuous confines of his clothing, yank her slacks down her long legs and thrust himself deeply inside her. His body screamed for release, but he set his teeth and fought the overwhelming barbaric urge to claim her with aggression.

He straddled her then, reached for the clasp of her slacks and unhooked it. Her eyes, glazed with passion, lifted to his. Slowly, he inched the zipper down, then slid his hands under the fabric and eased the garment off.

She arched upward, but he gripped her hips in his hands and stilled her. "Don't move," he said hoarsely.

If she moved, he'd forget his vow to take his time, to be careful with her. He wanted to pleasure her, knew that she would take him now, that he could rip away her clothing and make her his. But he held back, determined to control the thrashing beast inside him. The effort made sweat break on his brow, made his throat tighten and his breath harsh.

Slowly, he removed her slacks, felt her tremble when he ran his fingertips down her thighs, her calves, her ankles. Shoes and slacks fell to the floor, and she lay before him naked, except for the small triangle of white lace.

His heart slammed in his chest at the sight of her.

Her glorious thick, dark hair fanned across the pillow. Her skin was the color of fine ivory, her breasts, firm and full, the rosy peaks made for a man's touch. For *his* touch. Her legs were long, her waist slender, her hips curved.

"You're so beautiful."

Her lashes fluttered down, and a blush colored her cheeks. She raised an arm to cover herself, but he moved over her, brought her hand to his mouth and kissed each finger, moved to her wrist and touched his tongue lightly to her pulse, felt the furious beating of her heart. He moved up her arm, tasted her silky skin. She moaned when he nibbled at the juncture of her elbow, squirmed under him when he nipped the sensitive spot with his teeth.

She arched up, offering herself, and he turned his attention back to her breasts, caressed the soft flesh in his palms, then took one pebbled nipple in his mouth and sucked. She gasped, moaned deeply and dragged her fingernails over his shoulders, then raked her hands through his hair.

"Dylan, please…hurry…"

Moving his hand down her smooth, flat belly, he cupped her, then slid under lace and dipped into the wonderful, moist heat of her body. The small sound she made deep in her throat, wild and primitive, aroused him beyond anything he'd ever known. With his mouth still on her breast, he stroked her, slowly increasing the pressure.

When he knew she was ready for him, he quickly moved away, stood at the foot of the bed as he stripped off his clothing. He kept his gaze on her;

she kept hers on him. Her eyes widened at the sight
of him standing before her, naked and aroused. He
circled her ankles with his hands, moved up her legs,
slowly spread them. She quivered under his touch,
bowed her neck and bit her lip when he bent and
kissed the back of her knee.

He moved up her leg, gripped her hips with his
hands and lowered his head to the soft feminine
mound at the V of her thighs. She squirmed under
him, made a frantic sound and clutched at his shoulders. Through the soft silk, he nipped lightly, then
gently kissed.

She rose up, nearly sobbing. "Dylan, please, *now.*"

Knowing that he was too close to the edge himself,
he rose over her, ripped the small scrap of silk from
her hips, then thrust himself inside her, hard and fast
and deep.

When she cried out from distress, not pleasure, he
froze.

"Emily—"

"Don't stop." She wrapped her legs around him.
"Please, don't stop."

When she arched up and moved against him, the
last tiny thread of rational thought snapped. She
sheathed him in the tight, hot glove of her body and
he lost himself completely. Blood pounded in his
head, through his veins. Need, raw and primitive,
more powerful than anything he'd every experienced,
consumed him.

He felt the first shudder radiate from her body into
his, then heard her startled cry. She trembled, tight-

ened around him as the convulsions overtook her. His own release came, wave after crashing wave, as savage as it was fierce.

Still shuddering, both of them struggling to find their breath, he rolled to his side and held her close.

How long they lay there in each other's arms was difficult to tell. It seemed to Emily as if time had slowed, or quite possibly stopped altogether. She lay with her head on Dylan's chest, listened to the strong, steady beat of his heart. Her own heart was still racing, her breathing still quick. A sense of weightlessness filled her, made her feel as if she were floating.

She'd heard women talk about such things, but she'd never dreamed, never imagined making love could be like this. Never knew that a man's touch could make her completely lose control, turn her body inside out and expose every nerve, that pain and pleasure were so intertwined they became one.

But in spite of her inexperience, she was certain that what had just happened was not ordinary lovemaking. It couldn't possibly be, she thought. Her body still hummed, her mind reeled. Emily was certain that no other man could have brought her to that place, no other man could have come close.

Only Dylan.

The one man she could never have. The one man who would never want her after he learned the truth.

"Are you all right?" he asked, his voice strained, edged with concern.

Nodding, she pressed her lips to his chest, felt the ripple of hard muscle under her mouth. "Yes."

But she wasn't all right. Reality began to seep in, guilt settled over her like a heavy gray blanket.

Closing her eyes, she drew in a long, slow breath. *What am I going to do?* she asked herself. *Dear God, what am I going to do?*

But she knew. In her heart, in her soul, she knew exactly what she had to do.

He felt her pulling away from him, knew that he needed to say something, something significant, but he wasn't certain what. That he wouldn't have taken her if he'd known she was a virgin? That he was sorry he'd made love to her?

No. It would be a lie to say those things. Because even if he had known, he was certain he would have made love to her anyway. Because he wasn't sorry. He'd wanted her from the first moment he'd laid eyes on her, had been determined to take her to his bed. The fact that no man had taken her before him did not change what he'd felt.

And if he were to be completely honest with himself, he was glad she hadn't been to another man's bed. He felt a smug satisfaction that he was her first. He realized it might complicate matters when she remembered who she was, but they would deal with that then.

No woman had ever given him pleasure like that before. It wasn't her innocence, he'd been lost to her long before he'd realized that. It was her. Emily. The skim of her fingertips over his cheek, the brush of her mouth on his shoulder, the soft sounds she'd made while he'd loved her. Every kiss, every touch, every sigh, had spurred a need in him that went beyond the physical. He wasn't certain he liked it, but he knew it was something he would have to confront.

For now, he was content to hold her. Her heart had settled to a steady beat, and her breathing had slowed. When she slid one long leg over his to move away from him, he felt the need rear up in him again. He carefully forced it back down. As much as he wanted to slip inside her body again, as much as he wanted to bring her to the edge, then take her over, he knew she would need a little time.

He sighed, rubbed a soothing hand over her arm. "I do believe we settled the issue of whether or not a husband might be waiting for you."

She stiffened at his words, then turned her face into his chest. When he felt the warm moisture of her tears, he frowned, then took her chin in his hand and forced her to look at him.

"I thought that would ease your worry," he said, confused by her reaction, then realized that might not be why she was crying. "Or are you upset that you've lost your virginity to me?"

"No. It's not you," she whispered. "It's me. What I've done, it's wrong."

His frown deepened. "It's done, Emily. We're both adults. I wanted you, you wanted me. Why is that so wrong?"

She moved away from him, reached for her blouse beside the bed and pulled it on, then her slacks. He sat, dragged a hand through his hair and felt a flicker of annoyance that she hadn't answered him, that she had already turned cold, even when the rumpled sheets beneath them were still warm.

He watched as she moved to the French doors in the bedroom and stared out. He heard the distant screech of the seagulls, the crash of the waves below, waited impatiently for her answer.

"Bridgewater," she said unexpectedly.

"Bridgewater?"

"That is my name. Emily Bridgewater."

Something in her voice sent warning signals, chilled his blood and set his teeth on edge. He slid from the bed, reached for his trousers. "You've remembered your name?"

She turned to him, glanced away at the sight of him standing there naked. "I'm a school teacher at Clarton Elementary in West County."

"In Marjoco?" He'd heard of the town on the island to the west, though he'd never been there.

"Yes. I live there with my grandmother, Olivia Bridgewater."

He kept his gaze on her as he pulled on his pants and closed the zipper. "You've just remembered all this?"

"I've always known who I was," she whispered. "From the first day."

"What the hell are you telling me?"

"I've lied to you." Her voice trembled. She closed her eyes, then drew in a breath and opened them again, met his gaze. "I've lied to you about everything."

Nine

"**Y**ou've been lying to me?"

Dylan's words, spoken with such icy calm, such control, shivered up Emily's spine. He moved toward her, kept his dark-blue gaze locked on hers. Breath held, she steeled herself for whatever might happen next. She'd listened to her heart and made a decision.

There was no turning back now.

"Yes."

Once, on a wildlife show, Emily had seen a cougar corner a deer. Muscles coiled, body stiff, its entire being focused on its prey, the cougar had approached the deer the same way Dylan now approached her.

As strong as the temptation was, she didn't back away; as weak as her knees felt, she willed herself to stand firm, to face him down. To accept the consequences.

Still, when he moved into her space, when she felt the heat of his body, caught the musky scent of his skin, saw the anger glinting in his narrowed eyes, her legs trembled.

If he hadn't grabbed her, reached out and roughly snatched her arms, she was certain she'd be lying on the floor at his feet right now.

"The accident," he said tightly. "My car striking you."

"It was no accident," she whispered raggedly.

The single word he uttered was coarse and to the point. "Why?"

"I—I had no choice. I swear to you—"

"A person always has a choice, Emily." His hands tightened on her arms, and he shook her. "Always."

She winced at the pain radiating up her arms. "They kidnapped my grandmother."

Dylan went still. His eyes narrowed to slits. "Who?" he demanded. "Tell me."

"I—" She struggled to breathe, to see past the stars beginning to swim in front of her eyes. "I don't know who they are," she gasped. "Except for the man who brought me up to the mountain road, I never saw anyone's face. I was contacted by phone, by a man named Frederick. He told me they would kill my grandmother if I didn't do exactly as he said."

"And what *exactly*," he ground the word out, "did he tell you to do?"

"To…to get close to you."

"Well, Miss Bridgewater," he said, yanking her close, "I commend you. You've certainly accomplished that part of your mission well, haven't you?"

He released her suddenly, and she stumbled against the French doors, heard the rattle of glass and wood where her back struck the jamb. Like a hot arrow, pain shot through her shoulder.

"Did you think that having sex with me would lessen your punishment if you were caught?" he said tightly. "Is that why you came to my bed?"

"No." She shook her head. "I never intended this to happen. I thought I could do what they'd asked of me without…being intimate."

Unrelenting, he stood over her, his fists at his sides. "Why you, Emily? Why did they choose you?"

"I don't know how they found me, but they told me I resembled someone you were in love with once, a woman named Katherine."

"Katherine was the daughter of one of my father's aides. I was eighteen, she was twenty-one. Love had nothing to do with our relationship." He shook his head and swore. "Where the hell are these idiots getting their information, bathroom walls?"

He whirled away, took three steps, then whirled back again. "What were you supposed to do once you got inside the palace?"

"Get inside your suite. They gave me the security code to your alarm panel and the combination to your safe."

"My safe?" The fury in his expression continued

to darken. "How did they get the combination to my safe?"

"I don't know, I—"

"Don't lie to me, dammit." He moved in closer again, grabbed her chin in his hand. "I'll hear the truth now, Emily. All of it."

She swallowed the thickness in her throat, blinked back the moisture burning her eyes. "I'm telling the truth. The only thing I know is that there are papers inside your safe they want, documents I was supposed to steal and bring to them."

"Which documents? What is it they want?"

His face was only inches from hers, a face that had been smiling and loving only a few minutes ago. She knew that he would never look at her that way again, that from now on there would only be hatred and disgust.

"Diamonds." She damned the tear that slid from the corner of her eye. "They said your family has their diamonds, that the documents have the information they need to get them back."

"Fools and idiots." On an oath, he released her, then grabbed his shirt lying on the bed and pulled it over his head. He began to pace. "You said you never saw anyone's face except for the day on the mountain road. Does the man have a name?"

"Sutton." Emily rubbed at her arms, knew she was shivering, but couldn't stop herself. "I'm certain that isn't his real name, but I can describe him. And he was here, at the palace, yesterday when we were standing on the balcony above the ballroom. It was right after you—"

Kissed me, she nearly said, but quickly bit the words back. She couldn't think about any of that now, couldn't let herself remember the passion they'd shared. If she did, she'd surely fall apart.

Eyes narrowed, Dylan stopped his pacing and stared at her. "One of the Black Knights came here? To the palace?"

"Black Knights?" Emily pressed a hand to her throat. She'd heard of the subversive group that had been responsible for numerous attacks on Penwyck, but she'd had no idea they were the ones who'd taken Olivia. "The Black Knights have my grandmother?"

Unable to hold herself up any longer, she sank to the floor. Ice filled her veins. Everyone knew that the Black Knights were ruthless, that they would stop at nothing to get what they wanted.

"He was with the tour that came into the ballroom," she said quietly, her mind numb. "That's why I was so frightened. The men who took my grandmother told me they'd be watching me, that they would know my every move if I tried to get help or go to the police. When I saw Sutton, I was afraid he'd come there to talk to me."

Shaking his head, Dylan raked a hand through his hair. "How were you supposed to contact them?"

"I have a phone number to call. I'm supposed to find a public or pay phone and check in with them tomorrow."

"Then that's what you'll do," he said coldly and reached for the phone on the nightstand beside the bed. He punched in a number, kept his gaze lasered on her while he waited. "Send three men to the cliff house," he said into the receiver. "Tell Monteque we have to meet immediately. I'll be in his office in twenty minutes."

He hung up the phone and walked toward her. Anger glittered in his eyes. The Dylan she'd known was gone. In his place was a fierce, bitter man.

"Have you any proof?" he asked tightly. "Anything we might use to find where these men are hiding?"

"I taped our first phone conversation on my answering machine. I hid the tape in a safety deposit box in the First National Bank in West County. The key is—"

"We won't need a key." He stared down at her. "I have men coming to watch the house. You will stay here until I decide what to do with you."

He picked up his shoes, then strode toward the door.

"Dylan," she called out to him. He stopped, but did not turn. "Please believe me. I'm sorry. It was never my intention for anything to…for us to—"

"Save it," he said sharply. "I'm sure you'll understand if I don't believe a damn thing you say at this point. And as far as your intentions, Emily, you know what they say about the road to hell."

Hot tears slid down her cheeks, but she held her head up, watched him leave the room. He paused at the door again, as if he had a thought, and glanced over his shoulder. "Don't try to run away, Emily. I will find you if you do."

"I won't run," she said evenly. "It's my grandmother I'm worried about. I don't care what happens to me.''

''That's makes two of us, then.''

His words cut like broken glass; she closed her eyes against the pain. She didn't blame him. How could she possibly blame him? She deserved his anger, his disgust and more.

He walked away, and Emily heard the front door close a moment later. Once more she could hear the screech of the seagulls and the surf pounding the rocks below the cliff. Only it wasn't as it had been before. Everything was different now. Everything had changed.

Had she made a horrible mistake by telling him? she wondered. Had her honesty sealed not only her own fate, but her grandmother's, as well?

Too exhausted to think, she dropped her head into her hands and prayed that if Dylan would not forgive her, he would at least help her.

It took less than an hour to assemble the leaders of Penwyck's Royal Elite Team. Admiral Monteque, Duke Carson Logan, Pierceson Prescott and Sir Selywyn Estabon, all powerful, rich, impressive men.

They were men to be trusted, Dylan knew. Men in whom his father had complete confidence. They were intelligent and brave, fearless men who had proven their valor time and time again. They had their own code, their own rules, but their goal was the same: protect their country and their king at all costs.

The men had listened quietly and intently when

Dylan had presented the few facts he'd learned from Emily. Olivia Bridgewater had been kidnapped, her life threatened if Emily did not do what the men told her, which was to get close to the king's son and steal information regarding the diamonds from his safe.

"Does she know how the Black Knights gained knowledge of your alarm code and safe combination?" Monteque asked.

Dylan shook his head. "I'm guessing it's either an inside source or they've somehow managed to tap into the main computer controlling all the alarm pads. As far as my safe is concerned, I don't have a clue. No one knows that combination but me."

"I'll have one of my men do a security sweep right away," Carson Logan said. "A well-placed camera might be the culprit."

It enraged Dylan, the thought of someone bugging or wiring his room. But not as much as Emily's deceit had enraged him.

I've lied to you about everything.

Her words still rang in his head. How could he have been so stupid, so foolish? he'd asked himself a hundred times since he'd left the cottage.

She'd been so convincing, so clever in her ruse. Beautiful, innocent Emily. Sweet, vulnerable Emily.

Lying, deceitful Emily.

"Dylan?"

He snapped himself out of his thoughts, annoyed he'd let himself stray from what needed to be done now. He looked at Carson, realized that the man had been talking to him. "What?"

"I'm going to bring in my two best men to cross-examine the woman. Would you like to be present?"

"No." He didn't dare. He was wound too tightly to be close to Emily. He wasn't certain he would be able to control his emotions if he was in the same room with her. "I have other things to attend to. Keep me informed."

"Yes, sir."

"Would you like me to follow up on the tape in her safety deposit box?" Selywyn Estabon asked.

Dylan nodded. "When you retrieve it, bring it directly to me. Check the security tapes on all the tours given yesterday, as well. Miss Bridgewater claims she can identify one of the men in a tour group as the man who took her up on the mountain road. Have her review the tapes and see what you can find out."

Dylan stood, signifying the end of the meeting. With a quiet scraping of wooden chairs on a hardwood floor and the shuffling of papers, the rest of the men rose, as well.

"What do you want us to do about the grandmother?" Pierceson Prescott asked.

Dylan looked at Prescott. The man was impressive in stature and build. And, like the rest of the Royal Elite Team, trained in combat and the martial arts. Dylan glanced at the other men in the room. Each of them had their specialty, their own expertise they brought to an assignment. The room was taut with tension, everyone eager to get started.

"I want you to find out where those cowards are keeping the woman," Dylan said evenly. "Then we'll bring her back, alive."

"We?" Prescott frowned. "But, surely you don't mean that you intend to—"

"That's exactly what I intend." His jaw set, Dylan scanned the other men's startled faces. "If anyone has a problem with that, say so now."

The men exchanged glances, smiled, then Prescott stepped forward and bowed. "Of course not, Your Royal Highness. We would be honored."

Dylan nodded, then looked at the clock on the wall. "I expect to be briefed on every detail, no matter how small. We'll meet back here at nineteen hundred hours."

The room emptied. Alone, Dylan walked to the water cooler and filled a paper cup. He stared at the clear liquid for a long moment, then downed the contents.

On the drive back down from the cliffs, he'd been too angry, his pride too wounded, to think clearly. The very thought that Emily was connected to the Black Knights...

Swearing, he crushed the cup in his hands and hurled it into the trash can.

In his mind, he'd gone over and over that first day, when his limo had struck her. The image of the car hitting her was etched in his brain, but he needed to go back farther, to remember what had happened before. He closed his eyes, replayed the incident in slow motion, forced himself to remember details...

He and Liam had been discussing a hand of poker...*Let me win?* Liam had said, laughing, but his next sentence had been cut short when the bicyclist had suddenly appeared in the road. *Watch out!* Dylan had screamed. But it was too late. Liam had slammed on the brakes....

Dylan concentrated on that moment, that split second before the limo had struck Emily. He froze that moment in his mind....

She'd worn a white, short-sleeved blouse...long, blue denim skirt. Her head had snapped around at the sight of the car barreling down on her, skidding out of control. Her eyes had widened in terror, her dark hair had flown wildly around her pale face....

He stiffened then, remembering a detail he hadn't considered before: her cheek, right under those frightened eyes, had been bright red.

As if someone had used a fist on her only seconds before.

Sutton.

Dylan's own hands tightened into fists. Emily had said that the man had been up on the road with her. It appeared that he'd struck Emily before sending her out in front of the limo. Whether to make her comply with his demands or to make the accident appear worse, Dylan wasn't certain.

Either way, Dylan looked forward to coming face-to-face with the bastard, was anxious to see how the man could handle himself when he wasn't beating up women and kidnapping old ladies.

"Dylan?"

He glanced over his shoulder at the familiar voice, then turned and nodded. "Mother."

She stepped into the room and closed the door quietly behind her. Her cashmere suit was the color of sand, her low-heeled shoes a shade darker. She wore her dark hair up today, emphasizing not only her long, graceful neck, but the simple diamond earrings her husband had given her on their twenty-fifth wedding anniversary, along with a diamond necklace, simple diamond brooch and simple diamond bracelet, all handcrafted by the palace jeweler.

Since the day Dylan had returned to Penwyck, he'd noticed his mother had worn at least one piece of the ensemble of jewelry every day. Neither his mother nor his father had ever shown great sentimentality, and yet Dylan realized that his mother had worn the jewelry these past weeks to please her husband, to show him in her own way how much she cared for him.

There were people who speculated on the sincerity of the king and queen's marriage, whether theirs was truly a happy union, but Dylan knew in his heart that his parents deeply loved one another.

There was concern in Marissa's deep-blue eyes as she gazed at her son. "Sit, Dylan, and tell me what's happened."

He pulled a chair out for his mother first, then sat across from her. He started at the beginning, explained how Emily's accident and amnesia had been a farce and that through coercion, she'd been part of a plot to gain access to the palace in order to steal information from his safe.

"I have her under guard at my cottage," he told Marissa. "She'll be cross-examined to determine if she's telling the truth."

"Of course she's telling the truth," Marissa said with a dismissive wave. "She has no reason to lie now, especially with her grandmother's life at stake. Have you any leads on where the Black Knights might be keeping the poor woman?''

He shook his head. ''We're hoping to be able to do a reverse trace on the original phone call Emily received at her house, or possibly find a clue in the tape she recorded. She's also supposed to check in with them every few days, so we might be able to find a lead there.''

Marissa nodded her approval. ''You've handled this extremely well, son. Especially considering the circumstances and your own involvement.''

''I have no involvement,'' he said firmly.

''Ah.'' The smile she gave him, that all-knowing smile that mothers seemed to be born with, annoyed the hell out of him.

''And you've spent every possible minute with her and taken her to your cottage for what reason?''

He straightened, met his mother's sharp blue eyes. ''None of that is relevant to this investigation, Mother.''

''Isn't it?'' She tilted her head and studied him. ''Do you deny you care for her very much?''

Maybe he *had* cared for her, before he knew she'd deceived him. But whatever he'd felt no longer mattered. Other than what they could learn from her, he was done with the woman.

In any event, he had no intention of discussing that part of his life with his mother.

''She lied to me,'' he said, ignoring Marissa's question. ''She lied to all of us.''

"She did not lie to hurt anyone," Marissa said gently. "She lied to protect someone she loved."

He shook his head. "I fail to see the difference."

"Do you?" She lifted one finely arched brow. "So these past two years you've been gone, you've been traveling in Europe and staying with friends, have you?"

"I—" *She knows,* Dylan realized. Somehow his mother had found out where he'd truly been and what he'd been doing. But how? How could she *possibly* know? "What do you mean?"

Marissa sighed. "Never mind. You have other things to think about now. But when the time is right, Dylan, you and I have much to talk about."

She stood, then moved beside him and pressed a kiss to his temple. "I once read somewhere," she said softly, "that a woman loves with all her heart and a man with all his strength. You, my son, have much strength. Use it wisely."

Stunned by her words, Dylan watched his mother leave the room. He stared at the closed door for several long moments. What nonsense was she spouting about love?

Love had nothing to do with this situation at all. He might have let lust cloud his thinking, and he would certainly plead guilty to foolishness and stupidity, but love?

He sighed and shook his head. Women were dreamers, full of fantasies and illusions. Men saw reality and facts. They did not let emotions rule their decisions.

He would need to see Emily again, he knew. There

were still questions unanswered, pieces of the kidnapping and blackmail scheme that needed to be fitted together, things that he wanted to hear from her directly.

But he wouldn't let her close again, he told himself. He'd made an error in judgment with the woman once, and he'd be damned if he'd make that same mistake again.

Ten

It shamed Emily how well she was treated over the next week. Every morning, at eight o'clock, a fresh bag of groceries was delivered to the cottage. Clothes had been packed and sent in trunks, along with a bag of bath and hair and makeup items. The television, VCR and DVD players in the cottage all worked and Dylan had a wide and varied selection of movies in his collection, along with a well-rounded library of novels and books.

There were no bars on the windows, no locked doors, and no one stopped her when she walked along the cliffs every afternoon.

Nevertheless, there was no doubt she was a prisoner here.

Two shifts of three men in civilian attire patrolled the cottage grounds twenty-four hours a day, their guns hidden neatly under the sporty cotton jackets they wore. During the day, they strolled casually about, smoked and talked quietly amongst themselves. To anyone passing by, it would seem as though they were all out on holiday for a few days, enjoying a bit of fresh air by the ocean.

Nothing could be farther from the truth.

She glanced out the small window beside the front door. Thirty yards from the cottage, at the edge of the forest, a large, white trailer had been hauled in on the back of a pickup truck, a headquarters of sorts, she supposed. The men watching her ate and slept there, and when other men came up from the palace, they all gathered inside the trailer to hold meetings.

Two men she knew only as Westbrook and Gibbons had questioned her endlessly the first three days. They'd videod and tape-recorded every session. She'd requested a lie-detector test, but no one had given her one. They'd simply scribbled a note that she had made the offer. After those three days, no one else had come, and if not for the men outside watching her and the food deliveries, she might have thought they'd forgotten her altogether.

Especially Dylan, she thought, pressing a fist to her chest. He'd told her before he'd left her that she no longer mattered to him. Clearly he'd meant it.

But in spite of the heartache, in spite of the problems she'd caused the palace, she wouldn't have changed a thing. To save her grandmother, she'd do it all over again.

Emily had called her contact several days ago at

her scheduled check-in time, but the man who'd answered the phone would not let her speak to her grandmother. Though he had insisted that Olivia was sleeping, that she was fine, Emily had felt sick to her stomach with worry. She prayed the Black Knights had not hurt her grandmother in any way, and that Dylan's men would find her in time.

They had to, she told herself, refusing to consider any other option.

A blast of wind buffeted the cottage and howled down the chimney. Outside, tree branches swayed and a dust devil, carrying bits and pieces of wood and leaves, whirled past the window. Two of the guards walked by, hands dipped deep in their jacket pockets. Earlier, the day had been warm, but dark clouds were quickly moving in. There was no mistaking that tonight would be cold and wet.

With a sigh, she moved away from the window. As comfortable as her surroundings were in the cottage, she would have preferred a jail cell. Here, everywhere she turned she saw Dylan, felt his presence as surely as if he were standing before her. And if the days weren't bad enough, there were the nights.

It was impossible to lie in the same bed where they'd made love and not think of him. Impossible not to remember the passion they'd shared. The urgent, hot press of his mouth on hers, his hands—his magical, clever hands—gliding over her skin, arousing, destroying, consuming her with every masterful stroke, every skillful, breath-stealing caress. To think that she would never know such ecstasy again ripped at her heart.

But she wasn't sorry she'd given herself to him. There were so many things she was sorry for, but never that. She'd fallen in love with him. Her guilt and fear had clouded her feelings, made her deny them even, but she knew she'd loved him from the first moment he'd gathered her in his arms and laid her so gently in his car.

She did love him, even though she knew he could never love her back. Not after what she'd done. She would have to learn to accept that the man she loved, would always love, despised her.

Pain, fierce and swift, staggered her, tightened the knot in her stomach. She pressed a hand there, closed her eyes and waited for the nausea to roll through her.

She needed to keep busy, keep her hands and mind occupied. Sucking in a deep breath, she headed for the kitchen.

Damn the rain.

It fell in sheets of black ice, weighted his windshield wipers and battered the roof of the car. A bad night to be out on a narrow, winding mountain road, Dylan thought, his hands tight on the steering wheel, his eyes focused intently on the asphalt in front of him. A bad night to be out, period.

So what the hell was he doing here then?

He'd told himself before he'd driven up here that it was his responsibility to oversee every aspect of this…situation. He'd been working closely with the Royal Elite Team this past week. Every lead, no matter how small or unimportant it might have appeared, had been investigated, turned inside-out, then examined ten different ways.

Emily's deposition, plus the answering-machine tape that had been recovered from her safety deposit box, had supported everything she'd confessed to a week ago. Though she'd admittedly lied about not knowing who she was or anything about her past, it appeared everything she'd told them these past few days had been true. Westbrook and Gibbons had done an extremely thorough job of questioning her. The men had been impartial and demanding, relentless in their quest to obtain every detail not only of Emily's encounter with the Black Knights and the men named Sutton and Frederick, but every detail of her life in general.

The first time he'd watched the tapes, the feelings he'd thought he'd controlled resurfaced. Anger, like a vicious beast, clawed inside his chest. Hurt, sharp and fierce, stabbed at his gut. Disbelief swelled in his throat.

He'd watched the tapes again and again, and strangely, every time he did, his anger at Emily had slowly subsided. Like water dripping on a stone, bit by bit, drop by drop, his hurt eased. Disbelief turned to amazement.

He'd seen the love Emily felt for her grandmother every time she spoke her name. He'd heard it in her voice, seen it in her eyes and the tender way she'd touch the ring on her finger, a ring given to her by Olivia. And although he could not forgive Emily's betrayal, perhaps he could understand why she'd done what she had. Several months ago, Owen had been kidnapped, and though Dylan had been in Europe at the time and unaware of his brother's abduction, he knew that he would have done anything to see Owen safely returned.

Even the ridiculous accusation from his Uncle Broderick that Owen and he were not truly twins, that they'd been switched at birth with the real heirs to the throne who now lived in the States, none of that mattered to Dylan. No matter what the DNA tests ordered by his mother revealed, blood or not, Dylan knew that without hesitation he would sacrifice his own life for Owen's, or any other member of his family.

Wind rocked the car, and Dylan forced his attention back to the road. The ride was bumpy across the rain-gutted dirt drive to the cottage, and he swore more than once as he slowly maneuvered the Jaguar between the trees. Through the rain and darkness, he saw the lights, like a welcoming beacon, shining from within the small house. His pulse quickened at the sight, and he clamped his teeth, determined that he would remain indifferent.

He would question her, he told himself, then he would leave. The quicker the better.

The guard at the front door, Lieutenant Stevens, straightened when he caught sight of Dylan stepping out of his car. The man stood under the dripping eaves, holding a plate of food.

"Your Royal Highness," the guard snapped out.

"At ease, Stevens." Dylan sniffed at the food. It smelled delicious, certainly not the usual type of meal prepared by the men. "Why aren't you eating in the trailer if it's your meal time?"

"Well, sir, I—it's not exactly, I mean—"

"An answer sometime tonight would be appreciated, Stevens."

The guard swallowed. "Miss Bridgewater offered me a plate, sir. I accepted."

Dylan frowned. "I see. Does Miss Bridgewater always offer you meals?"

"No, sir." Stevens squirmed. "Just tonight, sir."

"Has Miss Bridgewater offered you anything else?"

The lieutenant thought hard. "A glass of milk and a cookie."

Milk and cookies. Dylan's mood darkened. What would she be offering next? To tuck them in at night?

"I'm sorry, Your Royal Highness," the guard said crisply. "If I broke policy—"

"Never mind, Stevens." Annoyed, Dylan simply shook his head. "Take your meal to the trailer. I'll call you to pick your shift back up when I leave."

Stevens hesitated, then nodded. "Yes, Your Highness."

Irritation tightened his jaw as Dylan watched the man hurry toward the trailer. He turned back to the front door and rapped sharply, waited several seconds.

No answer.

He knocked again, louder.

Surely she hadn't gone to bed yet. It was barely eight o'clock.

He felt a prickle of alarm. The reason he'd kept her out here and assigned guards was in case the Black Knights discovered their plan to use Emily had failed and attempted to take her out before she could testify against them.

He opened the front door, his senses alert, but all appeared fine inside. A cheerful fire warmed the room, and the most incredible smells drifted from the kitchen. Music, an Irish instrumental Megan had given him for his CD collection, flowed softly from the stereo.

He closed the door behind him, shrugged out of his jacket and hung it on a wall hook. It was like stepping into the pages of a novel...a husband coming home from a day's work, a hunger in his belly and a thirst in his throat.

He shook off the thought and moved toward the kitchen, froze at the sound of water running from the bath, felt his heart stop, then race.

She was taking a shower.

His throat went dry. She was naked. No more than twenty feet away. He could picture her standing there, under the steamy water, soaping her hands, then rubbing the foamy white bubbles over her arms, her breasts, then down her flat belly and lower still—

He jerked his mind away from that image and ground his teeth. Dammit, the woman had bewitched him! It was all he could do not to storm into the bathroom and take her right there in the shower, to push her wet, soapy body back against the cool tile and thrust himself inside her. He didn't even give a damn if he got his clothes off or not.

Sweat broke out on his brow. With something between a growl and a groan, he went into the kitchen, determined to satisfy at least one of his baser appetites.

Emily shut off the shower and quickly dried herself with a thick green towel. She lathered on a tuberose-scented lotion, dragged a comb through her tangled hair, then attacked the wet strands with several hot blasts from a blowdryer. She pulled on a pale-pink cotton nightie that Sally had packed for her, then the matching short robe.

The shower had eased some of the tension in her shoulders, at least, but she had a dull pounding in her brain. Several nights without sleep and worry over her grandmother were more than taking their toll.

And then there was Dylan.

It didn't matter how many times she told herself she would forget him, put everything that had happened between them behind her and face whatever punishment she was given, she still couldn't let go. Not yet.

At least she'd kept herself busy this afternoon. If there was one thing her grandmother had taught her, it was how to cook. After digging through the groceries she'd received that day and during the week, she'd settled on an endive salad with pecans and gorgonzola, a pastry-wrapped, wine-marinated roast, roasted rosemary potatoes, and three dozen frosted cake cookies—a recipe sworn to secrecy by all Bridgewater women.

When she'd offered a plate of food to the guard at the front door, he'd refused at first. But she'd been insistent she'd have to throw it away if he didn't eat it, so he'd relented. A few minutes later, she'd made two more plates and insisted he take them to the trailer or she'd have to dump them, as well.

Her grandmother had told her once that a woman who knew how to prepare that roast and her special cookies would have her choice of husbands.

Based on the requested seconds from the men, perhaps her grandmother was right.

But there was only one man she wanted—the one man she could never have. And the chances of him ever eating any food she prepared were somewhere between slim and none.

Shaking her head to loosen the curls already forming, she reached for a brush and walked into the living room to stand by the fire. She stared into the flames for a long moment, then bent at the waist and brushed her hair from the neck forward, tugging at the last few knots in the damp strands.

If only it were possible to untangle the mess she'd made of her life as easily, she thought with a sigh.

The sight Emily offered to Dylan hit him like a fist in his gut. Blood pounded in his ears as he stared at her backside; his heart slammed in his chest. He might have thought that she'd intentionally set out to arouse him, but she'd been deep in thought when she'd entered the room, her mind obviously miles away, and he was certain she hadn't noticed him sitting on the sofa.

He fisted the throw pillow under his hands and clamped his teeth tightly together. Through the thin robe she wore, the firelight outlined her slender body. Her legs, those endless legs, were spread slightly as she brushed at the wild mass of damp, dark curls. Her hips moved back and forth with every stroke of the brush.

He was hard instantly.

"Emily."

She straightened and whirled, her eyes round and her mouth open in a small O. A horrified expression crossed her face, then she moved quickly, belted her robe and pulled it tightly around her.

"Dylan." Her voice was breathless, tight. Her gaze dropped and she made a weak attempt to curtsy. "Your Royal Highness. I—I didn't know you were here."

"Obviously." He would have stood, but knew he wasn't ready yet. He didn't want her to know she could still affect him so strongly—and so quickly.

"What—what are you doing here?" She held the brush to her chest as if it were a weapon that might protect her against him.

"Sit down, Emily."

He needed her to sit. If she kept standing in front of that fire, her hair and body backlit by the flames, he wasn't certain he could hold himself together.

He'd thought of her too often this past week, remembered the feel of her soft skin, the sound of her sighs, the smell of flowers that surrounded her. She haunted his days, invaded his dreams at night.

He needed her out of his head, dammit. Needed her out of his system. He'd thought that coming here tonight would exorcise her from his mind, from his never-ending need to hold her again.

He'd been wrong. Terribly wrong.

She sat on the edge of a chair opposite him, back straight, body stiff, still clutching that damn brush. His gaze dropped to her long legs. Once again he had to force himself not to think about how desperately he wanted to slide his hands over her knees, part her soft thighs, then move between her legs and bury himself deeply inside her.

His gaze snapped back up to hers. He saw her fear, her confusion…and something else….

Desire.

He'd recognized the need, had seen it in her eyes before, when he'd kissed her, touched her. Made love to her.

He pressed his lips into a hard line. She may have used her womanly charm to snare him before, but it would not happen again. If she offered herself to him, perhaps he would indulge himself, he thought, though merely to relieve the tension tightly coiling in his body.

She looked down at the brush in her hand. "May I ask if you've learned anything regarding where my grandmother is being held?"

Thankful to have his mind back on palace business rather than his own raging libido, Dylan shook his head. "We've isolated an area, but until we have an exact location, we can't move. If we make a mistake, the Black Knights will know and immediately move out."

Emily closed her eyes, but not before he saw the anguish there. They both knew what would happen to her grandmother if the Black Knights found out that their plot and location had been discovered.

He could offer words of comfort, reassure Emily that Olivia would be fine, but he didn't. Not only because he didn't know if they could find her grandmother in time, but because he had no desire to console. Not with the taste of betrayal still lingering in his mouth.

Emily opened her eyes again, drew in a slow breath. "Why have you come here?"

Because I couldn't stay away, was his first thought, but he couldn't say that, wouldn't say it. The fact he now realized it was true only heightened his anger.

"I have some questions for you." He stood, walked to the fire, then turned to face her. "Regarding the man who was with you up on the mountain. The one you called Sutton."

His question seemed to surprise her. "But I've already told Westbrook and Gibbons everything I know."

"You said that he took you up there, waited until he received a phone call."

"Yes. I couldn't hear what he said, nor do I know who he spoke to. After he hung up, he told me to get on the bicycle and ride in front of your car."

"Is that when he hit you?"

She lifted a hand to her cheek, then glanced away and whispered, "Yes."

Bastard. He clasped his hands tightly behind his back, felt the knot in his stomach twist tighter. "Why didn't you tell that to Westbrook and Gibbons?"

"I—I don't know. Is it relevant?"

To me it is, he thought. He looked forward to

meeting this man. Soon. "Everything is relevant, Emily," he said sternly. "Is there anything else you've forgotten? Anything at all?"

"I—" She struggled to think. "I don't think so."

"Think, dammit!" He knew he'd shouted, but was too wound up himself to care. "What else have you forgotten?"

"Nothing." She shook her head. "I haven't forgotten anything."

Her eyes were bright with moisture as she lifted her gaze to his. The air shifted suddenly, grew heavy and taut. He felt it rush hot and wild through his blood. Every cell in his body seemed charged and alert.

"I remember everything," she said quietly. "How gentle you were when you picked me up and held me in your arms. The strength and warmth of your body when you carried me to your car."

"Stop this," he commanded.

"I remember that first thrilling moment when you brushed your lips against mine. You made me shiver. No man had ever done that."

He heard the rumble of thunder, wasn't certain if it was inside his head or the storm outside.

Eyes narrowed, he stalked toward her and grabbed her by the shoulders. "You're playing with fire, Emily. Stop this now, or I promise you that you will be sorry."

"Don't you know I'm already sorry?" she said raggedly. "So very sorry for everything I've done? Except you, Dylan. I will never be sorry for being with you."

A muscle jumped in his jaw. He felt the heat of

her body, caught the light, fragrant scent of her skin. His insides were twisting, his groin ached.

"I know you hate me," she whispered, the anguish heavy in her voice. "But you could never hate me more than I hate myself for lying to you and your family."

I don't hate you, he almost said, but couldn't find his voice. He felt as if a drum were beating in his head, in his chest. Heavy and loud, growing and growing, drowning out every thought but one: Emily.

With a growl, he crushed her to him. He caught her mouth with his in a savage, wild kiss that did not ask for submission, but demanded it. The brush she'd held in her hand clattered to the floor and her arms came around his neck, her need as fierce as his.

He lifted her, cupped her buttocks in his hands and pressed her firmly against his arousal. He felt more than heard the moan from deep in her throat, and the sound drove him over the edge.

With an oath, he swung her up in his arms and carried her to the bedroom, kicked the door shut behind him, then took her to his bed. He dropped her on the mattress, kept his eyes on hers as he yanked his shirt from his trousers, then opened the buttons.

"I want you," he said raggedly, "but understand, this means nothing to me. It will change nothing."

He saw the pain flicker in her eyes at his words, told himself he didn't care. He would take her, then walk away. And he would forget.

Emily watched Dylan strip off his clothes, then stand over her. His dark brows were drawn, his face stern as he stared down at her. Her heart leapt, then hammered in her chest. He was powerfully built, intimidating, his strength evident in the layers of hard, rippling muscles.

And he was fully aroused.

He frightened and excited her at the same time. Perhaps she should have tried to stop this, but she knew this might be the last time she ever saw him, the last time she might ever hold him. The last time she might ever have to love him. She understood for him it might be physical, but for her, it was so much more. Tonight, she gave him not just her body, but her heart.

He moved over her, dropped his mouth to hers and she could no longer think. She simply let herself feel. His hand tore at the knot on her belt, opened her robe, then slipped inside. He caressed the soft swell of her breast, dipped his head to suckle her through the thin cotton of her gown.

When he shoved her gown up and took the hardened tip of her nipple in his mouth, she bit her lip to keep from crying out. Intense pleasure braided in her belly, pulled tighter and tighter. She felt light-headed, dizzy. Moaning, she arched upward, raked her hands through his thick hair.

"I love you," she whispered hoarsely.

He went still at her words, lifted his head. Passion warred with anger in his dark-blue eyes as he stared at her. "Do not say that to me," he said fiercely. "I will have no more of your lies."

She took his face in her hands, carefully, and lovingly met his hard gaze. It would do no good to repeat the words to him. She would not try to convince, she knew he would not believe her. Instead, she rose to meet him, brought her mouth to his, felt his resistance slowly dissolve as her lips pressed to his.

In one swift move, he tore away the pink silk panties she wore, then covered her body with his. He entered her hard, fast, thrust himself deeply inside her. She lifted her hips, wanting him deeper still. With a groan, he grasped her buttocks and ground himself into her. She raked at his back, sobbing, the unbearable ache coiling tighter inside her with every thrust of his hips.

When her release came, she cried out, felt her body shatter into tiny, shimmering pieces. She held on, called out his name, opened her body and heart and soul to him. He shuddered against her in an explosion of primal heat, groaned deep in his throat as he spilled himself into her. She held him, knew that in a few minutes, when the passion cooled, he would not want her. She felt his heart beating fiercely against her own, pressed her lips to his shoulder, tasted the salt on his hot, damp skin.

She said nothing when he finally moved away from her. He said nothing.

He dressed quietly, then left her.

She heard the sound of the front door close, felt the cold creep over her, not from outside, but from her heart.

Eleven

Dressed in black, the men moved through the moonless night in pairs, ten teams in total. They surrounded the sprawling, three-story villa, blended in with the thick trees and lush foliage. Meticulously, carefully, they inched their way closer to the twelve-foot stone wall circling the compound.

Fog hung like a thick, gray blanket over the cold ground. The air was crisp and salty, swollen with moisture from the nearby ocean and the anticipation of combat. From the east, the lone howl of a distant wolf froze each man in place. An answering call from the west, and the soldiers hunkered down.

They waited.

His back pressed against the thick trunk of a tall cedar, Dylan waited along with the twenty-man team he'd assembled during the past three weeks. He'd

learned patience those two years he'd trained in Borovkia. The most successful assignments had been
won first with detailed strategy and caution, then
with courage and determination. He'd been taught to
plan, to wait, to listen—not only with his ears, but
with his gut. Those lessons had saved his life, and
the lives of the men he'd worked alongside more
times than he could count.

"Blackdog requests orders, sir," came a whisper
from the tiny radio in Dylan's ear.

"Are positions readied?" Dylan spoke quietly
into his mouthpiece.

"Affirmative."

"Five minutes." Dylan pressed a button on his
watch, knew that the other men did the same.

Five minutes.

A long time for a soldier waiting to move.

An eternity.

Dylan's family had objected to him leading this
mission, but when intelligence had finally discovered
the secluded seaside villa in Marjorco where the
Black Knights were holding Emily's grandmother,
Dylan had refused to be left behind. After everything
the bastards had done to his family, then black-
mailing Emily, Dylan vowed that tonight, once and
for all, the Black Knights would pay for their treach-
ery. By dawn's light, each and every man aligned
with the traitorous organization would be behind
bars or dead.

"Three minutes," Dylan heard the quiet voice in
his ear.

He knew that it might have taken years to discover

this secret location if not for Emily's cooperation. The phone calls she'd made every few days to her contact with the Black Knights to report her progress at the palace had been invaluable. Every call, Emily had insisted she be allowed to speak to her grandmother or she would not continue helping the men. Still, Emily's contact had always kept the calls under the time needed to trace the number.

Until the last phone call.

That call, when her contact had begun to hang up, Emily had blurted out that she'd finally been successful in seducing the prince, and that she would only need a few more days to gain his confidence and access to his safe. She then began to describe— in detail—*how* she had seduced Prince Dylan. Her explicit description of how she'd removed her clothes, how she'd slipped off her blouse, then her bra, how she'd touched herself, had greatly interested and momentarily flustered the man at the other end of the phone.

Lord knew, when Dylan heard the recording of the call, *he'd* been flustered, then annoyed that the intelligence team would also have to hear Emily's arousing account of seduction.

But the extra few seconds had gained Dylan's men the crucial time they needed to trace the call. He knew he had to put his own annoyance aside and simply concentrate on the task at hand, which was discovering where the Black Knights were hiding out.

Still, Dylan couldn't help thinking how easily Emily had lied to the man on the phone. He couldn't help remembering how easily she'd lied to *him*.

He hadn't seen her since the night they'd made love. But he would be the one lying if he said he hadn't wanted to see her. More than a dozen times he'd started for his car, intending to drive up to the cottage, torn between wanting to yell at her and wanting to kiss her.

But he would not allow himself those emotions. He did not trust himself to be alone with her and not drag her into his arms, then make love to her. So instead, he'd stayed away, had focused on helping discover the Black Knights' location and coordinating tonight's mission.

"One minute."

Adrenaline pumped through Dylan's veins, burned in his stomach. His muscles tightened, his breathing quickened. Forcing all other thoughts from his mind, he counted down with the rest of the men, then slipped out from his position behind the tree.

The men moved as one, inching their way closer to the wall. Two days' surveillance had revealed that the guards changed shifts at exactly nine o'clock. If Dylan's first wave of four men timed it right, each one of them could take out two guards at the same time, while the rest of the Royal Elite Team had two minutes to break inside the villa before an alarm would sound, then possibly another two minutes to find Olivia.

The lamp posts from inside the compound backlit the two guards on the wall changing shifts. Dylan watched as the men smoked and shared a joke while a dark figure—Captain Ian Alson—easily scaled the stone wall, then quickly disabled both startled men.

Dylan and his team were over the south wall in fifteen seconds, made a dash across the lawn, then climbed up a wrought-iron lattice and entered the villa through a pair of French doors. At that exact moment, if all went according to the plan, eight other men would be entering the house, as well.

Gun in his hand, Dylan listened, heard the sound of a laugh track from a television sitcom coming from the second room down.

Olivia's room.

Silently, Dylan directed the man with him to the end of the hall, then he moved to the room and knocked lightly. Without waiting for a response, he stepped inside, then locked the door behind him.

With her back to him, Olivia sat primly on a large white sofa in the living area, watching an old episode of a popular family comedy. She wore a bright pink housecoat and slippers, and she'd wrapped the sides of her short, curly silver hair in some kind of stretchy blue bandanna. Dylan scanned the room, noted a closed door that he knew would open into a bedroom and bath area. When he felt confident they were alone, he holstered his gun. "Mrs. Bridgewater?"

Olivia jumped at the sound of Dylan's voice. She turned, her eyes wide as she took in the sight of the black-uniformed, armed man suddenly standing in her room. She pressed a frail hand to her throat. "Oh, my heavens! You startled me, young man."

"I'm so sorry to disturb you like this, madam."

Dylan stepped into the room, forced himself to remain calm even as the distant sound of gunfire rang out. "But could I please trouble you to get dressed and come with me?"

"Whatever for?"

"Your granddaughter asked me to bring you home."

"Emily?" The woman furrowed her brow. "But Frederick told me that Emily's on her way tomorrow."

"There's been a change of plans, Mrs. Bridgewater." He walked quickly to the open balcony doors. He heard shouts from outside, another gunshot. He closed the doors, then turned back to Olivia and forced a smile. "Would you mind?"

"Well, I suppose not." Olivia stood, patted the bandanna around her head. "Dear me, it's been years since a handsome man spirited me away during the night. I'm not sure what to—"

The door broke open and a man rushed inside, waving a .357 Magnum. *Sutton.* Instantly, Dylan had his own gun in his hand and pointed at the man intelligence had identified as Damek Cutter, a vicious mercenary who'd been with the Black Knights for three years. This was the man who'd used his fist on Emily, Dylan remembered. His hand tightened on the cold metal in his palm, and he wished to God that Olivia wasn't standing between him and the mercenary.

"Drop it," Cutter roared.

Dylan held his gun steady. "Not a chance."

Cutter swung his gun and pointed it at Olivia,

whose face had paled. "Drop it, or I drop the old lady."

Olivia gasped.

Dammit. A muscle jumped in Dylan's jaw. He knew the bastard would do it. Lips pressed into a hard line, Dylan swung his gun away, then slowly lowered it to the floor.

"Wise decision, Dylan," came another voice.

A man stepped over the splintered wood and entered the room. Dylan glared at him. Anyone other than Dylan's immediate family would have thought the man was Dylan's father. He was identical to King Morgan in nearly every way.

"Hello, Uncle Broderick," Dylan said dryly. "Or should I call you Uncle Frederick?"

"Frederick is your uncle?" Clearly confused, Olivia glanced at Dylan, then back to Broderick. "Frederick, I demand you explain all this to me immediately."

"My dear Olivia, you are so naive." Broderick shook his head, then sighed. "It's all about money and power, my dear. I was born to have both, but my family stripped me of everything I deserve, everything that should have been mine, including my title."

"You'll have a new title now, Uncle, one you truly deserve." Dylan heard the sound of more gunfire, prayed his men would arrive in time. "It's called prison inmate."

"I'll never go to jail," Broderick said, narrowing his eyes. "I'm a Penwyck. A king!"

"You're a kidnapper and a blackmailer." Dylan

could see that his uncle truly had gone mad. "You used innocent women for your own selfish gains."

"When I stumbled upon Miss Bridgewater's picture in the West County newspaper, a candid snapshot of volunteers serving meals at a senior citizens' center, I was struck by her resemblance to that young woman you were so taken with several years ago, Miss Katherine Demasse. We needed to send someone inside the palace, but I knew I'd never get one of my men past security. But a beautiful woman—" Broderick smiled at what he thought was such a clever plan "—that was easy."

Dylan took a step toward his uncle, stopped when Cutter swung his gun back around. "Almost as easy as a jury deciding your fate. What do you think you'll get for treason and attempted murder along with your other crimes?"

"Enough!" Broderick leveled a dark, icy gaze at his nephew. "All we wanted were the diamonds. *We* mined them. *We* are the rightful owners."

"You mined them illegally, from a mine that belongs to the government of Penwyck." Dylan had to get Olivia out of the way if he was going to make a move, but he didn't know how without jeopardizing her life. "It's already been decided the diamonds will be sold and the money distributed to all the charities on Penwyck."

"Once your mother learns that I have her precious son," Broderick hissed, "I'll have what belongs to me within twenty-four hours."

At the sound of gunfire from inside the house, Broderick frowned, then quickly glanced at Cutter.

"Kill the old woman, then bring my nephew to the chopper pad. I've got a pilot waiting."

Cold pleasure lit Cutter's eyes and a smile tugged at the corner of his mouth as he narrowed his evil gaze down the barrel and aimed—

"My heart!" With a strangled cry, Olivia grabbed her chest.

Cutter and Broderick both hesitated, then watched as Olivia crumpled to the floor.

The momentary distraction was all Dylan needed. In one swift, fluid motion, he pulled a knife from his boot and sent it flying directly into Cutter's chest. The mercenary went rigid, then stared wide-eyed at the blade sticking from his chest. His face contorted with pain and fury, and he lifted his gun toward Dylan. Dylan dove, but the blast caught him in the upper arm. Pain and searing heat shot through his shoulder and chest. Behind him, the bullet exploded, then shattered the patio doors. Glass and wood scattered across the carpet.

Eyes still wide, Cutter went down on his knees, then fell back and lay still. Broderick turned to run, but two men, Logan and Monteque, stood at the door to stop him.

His heart pounding furiously, Dylan rushed to Olivia and gently rolled the woman to her back. "Mrs. Bridgewater!"

Olivia's eyes popped open. "Is it over?"

She was alive! Thank God. "Are you all right? Your heart—"

She waved a hand and sat. "Of course I'm all

right. A ruse, young man, to help you stop those blackhearts. Oh my heavens, you're bleeding!''

"I'm fine." Dylan ignored the intense pain spiralling up his arm and helped Olivia sit on the sofa. But when he stood, the room spun, while the walls seemed to close in. He tried to say something, but couldn't hear his voice over the shrill ringing in his ears. A man's voice, deep and blurred and very distant, said something to him.

Monteque?

He reached out a hand to steady himself, struggled against the black fog creeping over him. He thought of Emily, saw her face hovering above him, then her arms reaching out. He tried to lift a hand, but it was too heavy. His entire body was too heavy. And then she was gone, and only darkness was left.

"Please, come in."

Emily held the cottage door open as the two uniformed men removed their hats and stepped into the living room. They stood in a military stance, their faces blank and unsmiling.

Oh, God. Something's wrong, she thought, terribly wrong. Emily's heart slammed in her chest, but she held herself steady and faced the men.

"I'm Lieutenant Randall Molson," the taller of the two men said. "And this is Sergeant Quinton Cars."

Emily nodded at the men, but did not offer her hand. "Lieutenant, Sergeant. Would you like to sit?"

"No, thank you, Miss Bridgewater. That won't be necessary. But if you would…"

"No." She prayed her legs wouldn't give out on her. "Why don't you just tell me why you're here, Lieutenant Molson."

Emily swallowed the lump in her throat when the lieutenant hesitated and readied herself for the worse.

Please let my grandmother and Dylan be all right.

She fought against all the horrible scenarios that pinballed in her mind. They *had* to be all right, she told herself. She couldn't bear it if they weren't.

Since the last phone call she'd made to her contact at the Black Knights, there'd been no visits from Intelligence. Every time she thought of that phone call and the method by which she'd kept the man on the phone, her cheeks had burned. But she knew her vivid account of a fictional striptease had worked. They hadn't needed to tell her that they'd finally managed to trace the call, she'd seen the elation in the men's eyes.

Emily knew that if they'd found the location where the Black Knights were holding Olivia, a plan had been set in place. She also knew that any plan to capture the Black Knights was risky, that her grandmother would be in serious danger.

That Dylan would be in danger.

The past three days she'd paced the small cottage like a caged cat, had sensed that something was happening, even though no one had said anything to her.

And now these men had shown up.

She drew in a slow breath and waited. The lieutenant cleared his throat, then quickly clipped out, "Miss Bridgewater, we're here to drive you to the airport. At oh-ten-hundred, there's a flight that will take you to Marjoco, where you will be met by a driver who will escort you home."

Home? They were releasing her? Allowing her to go home?

"My—my grandmother?" She could barely get the words out, she was so frightened to hear the answer.

The hard set of the lieutenant's jaw softened. "Mrs. Bridgewater is anxiously awaiting your arrival, Miss Bridgewater."

She was alive! Her grandmother was alive!

"Is she—" Emily had to swallow the thickness in her throat before she could speak. "She's all right?"

"Yes, miss." The lieutenant smiled now. "Your grandmother is fine."

In her happiness, Emily nearly threw herself at the man, wanting desperately to hug someone. She clasped her hands tightly in front of her.

"Thank you," she whispered, closing her eyes. "Thank you."

And Dylan? Emily wondered. Where was he? Why hadn't he come with this news?

She opened her eyes, nearly asked the question, then stopped herself.

Because she knew the answer. He could never forgive her for what she'd done. Could never forget how she'd betrayed him.

It felt as if a steel band were squeezing her chest,

forcing the breath from her. She'd never see him again, never touch him again.

The enormity of it, the finality, clawed at her insides.

She pressed a hand to her stomach. He'd never know. "I—I can be ready in ten minutes," she said to Lieutenant Molson and the sergeant. She had nothing to pack. Nothing here belonged to her. Nothing at all. "Would you mind waiting outside?"

The men nodded, then joined the guards outside.

She just needed a minute alone. A few moments to gather herself together before she left.

Numbly, she walked around the room, ran her fingers over a pine tabletop, stopped to gaze at a picture of a teenage Dylan with his sister Anastasia on the deck of a sailboat, both of them smiling and happy, their dark hair windblown and tousled. She brushed her fingertips over a leather-bound copy of *Hamlet,* then *Atlas Shrugged.* She could smell him here, feel his presence.

She would never forget this place. It had been her sanctuary and her prison at the same time.

If Dylan were not a prince, if he were an ordinary man, she would fight for him. Plead with him to hear her out, make him understand why she'd done what she'd done. Convince him somehow that she loved him.

But he *was* a prince, a successor to the throne, even though he'd told her that he'd never be king, that his brother Owen would rule Penwyck when King Morgan stepped down.

Emily sighed and slowly shook her head. Prince

or king, it didn't matter. An elementary-school teacher from a tiny town in West County had no place in a palace. One day Dylan would marry a woman of title or royalty. They'd have children who would be princes and princesses. He would go on with his life. He would forget her.

She drew in a slow breath, smiled in spite of the tears burning her eyes. But she would never forget him.

Once again, she pressed a hand to her stomach.

Ever.

Twelve

———

"It's just a scratch, for God's sake. Will everyone stop hovering?"

Dylan lay in the infirmary bed, more than annoyed that almost his entire family, not to mention two nurses, had crowded into the room. If someone asked if they could fluff his pillow or bring him anything one more time, he was going to throw the whole lot of them out. Except for his mother and father. Not even he could throw King Morgan and Queen Marissa out of the room.

"He's been cranky since he was admitted yesterday," Anastasia whispered to Megan and Meredith.

"He's been cranky most of his life," Megan quipped back, but there was tenderness in her eyes, not malice.

"I heard that," Dylan snapped. "And I am *not* cranky, dammit."

"Of course you're not, dear." Marissa patted her son's hand. "Maybe some pain medication would calm you down."

"I don't *need* any pain medication," he lied. His arm hurt like a son of a bitch. "And I don't need to be calmed down, either. What I need is to get out of here."

King Morgan harrumphed from a chair beside the bed. "You've only been here twenty-four hours, son. Try five months in the hospital, then you've a right to complain."

"I…am…not…*complaining,*" he said through clenched teeth. "I've been examined and treated. There's no reason for me to be here any longer."

Marissa smoothed the crisp white sheets over the edge of the bed. "You have fifteen stitches and you lost a lot of blood, Dylan. Doctor Waltham wants to keep an eye on you for at least another day or two. If I have to, I'll post guards outside your door."

Dylan bit back the earthy swear word threatening to erupt, a word he never used in front of his mother. He recognized the tone in her voice, knew she wasn't bluffing. Until the doctor released him, Dylan knew he was a prisoner here.

Dammit.

It more than pricked his pride that he'd gotten himself shot and had passed out for a few minutes, but in light of the overall success of the mission, Dylan knew he had nothing to complain about. The Black Knights had all been rounded up and captured, and his uncle had been arrested. There'd been four fatalities, all of them Broderick's men, and only five casualties, including himself. Olivia Bridgewater had been escorted home safe and sound.

And Emily…

He knew that she had left the cottage, that per his orders, she'd been flown back to Marjoco and reunited with her grandmother. He told himself that he was glad she was gone. He could forget about her now, get on with his life. There was much to do to restore order in the palace. He had no time to think about a beautiful, dark-haired enchantress.

He hadn't mentioned Emily once since he'd returned, but he knew his mother and sisters had already guessed he wasn't as indifferent to the woman as he'd pretended to be. The last thing he wanted to do was discuss his feelings for Emily with his family.

Especially when he didn't know what those feelings were himself.

She hadn't asked to see him before she'd left. He told himself that he was glad, that he would have refused if she had asked to meet with him. Now that the Black Knights were apprehended and her grandmother was safe, what else was there to say between them?

And even as he asked himself that question, he knew the answer: *Everything.*

He scowled at the IV of antibiotics attached to his arm, cursed his imprisonment in this damn hospital room.

Neither he or Emily had been completely truthful

to each other, he realized. Neither one of them had been truly honest.

Perhaps it was time they were.

As if there weren't enough people in his room, the door opened and Owen came in. His wife, Jordan, and their four-year-old daughter, Whitney, followed, as did a white-gloved server carrying a silver tray loaded with filled champagne glasses.

Champagne? Dylan narrowed a gaze at his brother. Owen only grinned like that when he was up to something. Dylan glanced at his mother and father. They were grinning, as well.

King Morgan nodded at the server, who bowed and backed out of the room. Both nurses left as well.

What the hell was going on? Dylan wondered. He watched everyone in the room take a glass of champagne and raise it toward him. Something was definitely up.

Something big.

Clearly, he was about to find out.

Emily sat on the small sofa in her living room and stared at the suitcases she'd packed the night before. There were six in all, three for herself, three for her grandmother. Everything they'd need to live in the States for the next few months. Olivia had a cousin there, Veronica, whom she hadn't seen in twenty years. The woman owned a farm in Connecticut, and had been widowed for two years. When Emily had called Veronica and asked if she and Olivia could come for a visit, the woman had been thrilled and insisted they not only come, but that they stay as long as they wanted.

It had been a busy week getting passports, subletting their house and convincing Alba Huntley, the headmistress at Clarton Elementary, to agree to the ten-month leave of absence Emily had requested. But everything was ready now, everything in place.

She was ready, she told herself firmly. She had to be.

What choice did she have?

Emily rose and walked to the sliding glass door overlooking her postage-stamp-sized garden. A gray mist moistened the bricks of her tiny patio where empty clay pots waited to be planted with spring annuals and a two-foot plaster gnome with green pants, a blue shirt and a red pointed hat waved one hand in welcome. Daffodils and paper whites would push through the cold ground in another few months, Emily knew. She'd miss the riot of color from the tulips and larkspur, the sweet scent of roses and alyssum.

She'd miss so many other things. Her children at school, sharing tea with her neighbor across the street, the excitement of back-to-school night, holiday parties in the teachers' lounge.

Dylan.

She'd miss him most of all. For the past week, since she'd come home, she'd thought about him constantly. The nights had been the hardest, when the house was quiet and she lay in her bed, unable to sleep. How could she not remember the thrill of his hand on her skin, the press of his lips against hers? How could she not remember how perfectly their bodies had fit when they'd made love?

She'd never know that kind of love again, she was certain. After Dylan, how could she?

Turning from the patio door, she stared at the one-way plane tickets sitting on the table beside her phone. Their flight left in three hours. An emptiness consumed her, chilled her to the bone.

The sound of her grandmother singing an old English ballad floated in from the other room. She'd been so happy these past few days. It seemed as though her adventure with the Black Knights and her dramatic rescue had given Olivia renewed vitality. She hadn't appeared quite so confused, and she had more energy than Emily could keep up with.

Emily glanced at the wood-framed clock on the mantle over her brick fireplace. The taxi would be here soon. She really should gather sweaters and coats, turn off the furnace and walk through the house one more time to make sure she hadn't forgotten anything.

With a sigh, she picked up the tickets, glanced at the itinerary once more. The paper seemed to burn her fingers; heat radiated up her arm.

Dear God. The numbers and words on the paper blurred.

She looked up, eyes wide as she scanned the living room. Her pulse kicked, then quickened. And in that one moment, that split second of time, she knew.

She couldn't leave. No matter how much she wanted to run away, she couldn't. No place would be far enough.

And it would be wrong. Very wrong, for her to leave now.

Afraid that she might change her mind, Emily set her grandmother's ticket back on the table. Her hands shook as she firmly grasped her own ticket and ripped it in thirds, then walked to the fireplace and threw it inside. She stared at the shredded paper, felt the knots in her stomach slowly unwind and the weight in her chest lighten.

Almost giddy, she pressed a trembling hand to her lips. She had to tell her grandmother that she would be visiting Veronica by herself, that she could come back here, to West County, whenever she was ready.

Emily jumped at the sound of a solid knock on the front door. The taxi. She would ride to the airport with her grandmother and make sure she got on her plane all right, then she would return home and do what she knew she needed to do.

One way or another, whether he wanted it or not, she would see Dylan.

Whatever happened, so be it. But there would be no more lies.

The doorbell rang now, followed by another knock, louder this time. She hurried across the room, her mind racing with what lay ahead of her, a mix of fear and excitement. She opened the door.

And froze.

Dylan.

She stopped breathing, was certain her heart had stopped, as well. He wore a long black overcoat over black trousers and a blue, long-sleeved shirt that darkened his already deep-blue eyes. Those eyes stared at her now, pinned her to the spot. She simply stared back, too stunned to move.

Had she willed him to appear simply by thinking that she would see him again? What was the expression, "Be careful what you wish for?" A moment ago, there'd been so many things she'd wanted to say to him. And now that he stood here, her mind went blank.

"May I come in?"

There was no emotion in his voice, no expression on his face.

And still she couldn't move.

A light mist of rain covered his dark hair. Her fingers itched to brush the dampness away, to touch his face. Her heart started to pound, low and heavy, and she willed herself to breathe.

"Emily." There was an edge of annoyance in his voice. "I'd like to come inside."

She blinked, realized that she'd been standing here like a complete idiot. Taking a step back on weak knees, she curtsied. "Of course, Your Royal Highness. Please, come in."

He strode past her, his shoulders stiff, his stance formal. She turned to shut the door, noticed the four men in suits standing beside a black limousine.

Why had he come to see her so heavily guarded? she wondered.

Why had he come to see her at all?

Her heart slammed against her ribs. Had he come to arrest her? No one had ever specifically told her that she would not be sent to jail, but she'd assumed when they'd released her and sent her home that any charges against her had been dropped.

Trembling, she closed the door, turned to face him, then had to clasp her hands tightly in front of her for fear he would see her shaking.

He glanced at the suitcases, then frowned darkly at her. "Are you going somewhere?"

Not anymore, she wanted to say. But the edge of anger in his voice made her hold back. "Is there any reason that I should not?" she asked carefully.

"You did not answer me."

"My grandmother has a cousin in Connecticut." His terse manner confused her. "After everything that's happened, I thought a visit would be good for her."

He shook his head. "You cannot leave."

Dear Lord. So he *was* here to arrest her. She fought back the cold panic inching up her spine. "I—I've told you everything I know, Dylan." She cast her eyes downward. "Your Royal Highness."

"Have you?" He took a step toward her. "Before you run away, is there not still something that you should tell me?"

"The Black Knights have—"

"Dammit, this has nothing to do with the Black Knights. They no longer exist. This is about you," he said evenly. "And me."

Her gaze shot upward. Did he know? *No,* she thought, her mind racing. He couldn't possibly.

"Ah, so there *is* something." His voice softened, and he moved closer still. "I can see it in your eyes.

I'll have nothing less than the truth now, Emily. You owe me that much.''

She did. She owed him the truth, and so much more.

"Yes," she whispered. "I do."

"Tell me." He reached out, took her chin in his hand. "Tell me your feelings for me. Your true feelings.''

Her feelings for him? *That's what he wanted to know? Why he'd come here?*

Hope fluttered in the pit of her stomach, but she refused to give in to it yet, refused to let herself believe that he'd come here because he cared about her.

"I—I thought you came here to arrest me."

"Arrest you?" He furrowed his brow. "I suppose I could. If it means keeping you here.''

She swallowed hard, terrified that she might be misunderstanding what he was saying to her. "Does it matter to you, Dylan?" she asked softly. "If I stay or go?"

"It matters." He brushed his thumb across her cheek. "It matters a great deal."

"I was going to leave," she said quietly. His thumb stilled on her cheek; his eyes narrowed. "But I tore up my ticket and threw it in the fireplace.''

He glanced over his shoulder, saw that she'd told him the truth. The stiffness in his shoulders eased as he turned back to her. "Why?"

She leaned into him, kept her gaze level with his. "Because I love you."

She'd said those words to him before, the last time

they'd made love. But she knew he hadn't believed her. She prayed he'd believe her now.

"Dylan," she hurried on when he said nothing. "I understand there's no place in your life for me, but if you—"

He dragged her against him, caught her mouth to his. Startled, it took her a moment to respond, then her arms were around his neck, kissing him back.

"You love me," he whispered against her lips.

"I love you." She drew back, watched a slow smile spread over his face. Drawing in a deep breath, she stepped away, needed to put a little space between them before she told him everything. "And there's something else I—"

"Emily, have you seen my blue bonnet? I was certain I left it on my bed, but it's not there. Oh!"

Olivia stopped at the sight of the man standing in the middle of the living room with her granddaughter, then beamed. "Why, what a pleasant surprise! How delightful to see you again, young man. Emily, dear, you never told me that you knew—" Olivia hesitated, then frowned. "Heavens, I don't know your name, sir. How terribly ungrateful of me."

Flustered, Emily glanced from her grandmother to Dylan, then back to her grandmother. "You know each other?"

"Well, of course we do," Olivia said brightly. "I told you all about him, dear. This is the man who saved my life."

"Saved…your…life?" Emily's voice was barely a whisper. Wide-eyed, she stared at Dylan. "*You* were the soldier who saved my grandmother's life?"

"Took a bullet for me, he did," Olivia said solemnly, then marched up to Dylan. "Lean down here, young man, so I can thank you properly. I never did get a chance in all the commotion that night."

"It was an honor, Mrs. Bridgewater." But Dylan did as he was told and Olivia kissed him on the cheek.

Emily looked at Dylan, felt the blood drain from her face. She reached out to him, then quickly drew back, afraid she might hurt him. "You...took a bullet? Oh my God, Dylan. I didn't know."

A wave of nausea rose in her stomach. Her knees turned to water, and she might have gone down if Dylan hadn't scooped her up in his arms.

"Emily! You poor child. Are you sick again?" Distressed, Olivia clasped a hand to her throat. "I'll run and get a cold washcloth."

Dylan watched Olivia hurry out of the room, then looked at Emily. Her face was pale as a sheet, her eyes wide with distress.

"You were shot," she murmured. "You could have died."

"I'm fine, Emily," he assured her. "It was barely a scratch. What did your grandmother mean when she asked if you were sick again? Have you been ill?"

"Dylan, please." She closed her eyes. "Please put me down."

"Not until you answer me. What's wrong with you?"

"There's nothing wrong with me," she whispered. "Except..."

"Except what?" he asked impatiently.

Her eyes opened slowly and met his. "I...I'm pregnant."

"Pregnant?" he repeated hoarsely. "As in *baby?*"

"I don't believe there's any other kind. Please, put me down now."

In a daze, Dylan carried Emily to the couch and gently laid her on the cushions. He stared at her, still struggling to find his breath. He could feel his pulse thrumming in his temple, could hear the pounding in his ears.

A baby.

His baby.

A muscle jumped in his jaw. Slowly, carefully, he drew air into his lungs. "You were going to keep this from me?"

"I considered it." She sat, lay her head back on the cushions and sighed. "I knew you hated me—"

"Dammit, Emily, I—"

"Please, hear me out, Dylan," she said weakly. "I was certain that you could never forgive me for what I'd done to you and your family. I was worried you would resent or reject any child we made together."

Shaking his head, he dragged a hand through his hair. "I don't give a damn what you thought I felt. You had no right to—"

"Will you let me finish?" A little color had come back in her cheeks, though not much. "I said I considered it, that's all. But I knew I couldn't. Why do you think I tore up the plane ticket? I know that no matter what's happened, or how you feel toward me, this is your child, too. You have a right to make the decision if you want to be part of his or her life. I'll never pressure you, but I'm hoping you will want to, Dylan.''

"I found my bonnet!" Olivia announced cheerfully, then stopped at the sight of Emily sitting on the sofa. "Oh, dear me. The washcloth."

She turned promptly and left again.

Dylan clenched his teeth, resisted the urge to shake Emily. He stomped to the fireplace, counted to ten, then stomped back. "We'll be married right away."

Shock widened her eyes, then she firmly shook her head. "No."

"What do you mean, no?" he demanded. "You said you loved me. You're having our baby. I refuse to accept no."

"I won't marry you because I'm pregnant, Dylan."

"Emily, for God's sake. I'm not asking you to marry me because you're pregnant." Dylan reached into his pocket and pulled out a small, black velvet box. "I'm asking you to marry me because I love you."

He knelt beside her, opened the box and held it out. Emily went very still, stared at the large diamond solitaire, then lifted her gaze back to his.

"You…love…me?"

"Yes, I love you. I think I knew the first moment I laid eyes on you. I knew that you belonged to me, only to me. And me to you." He took her hand in his. "I came here today to ask you if you'd be my wife. If you'd sit beside me and be my queen."

"Your queen?" Her face had paled again. "I don't understand."

"My father is abdicating the throne. He has named me king."

"You…" Emily's eyes widened. "But Owen…"

"The DNA tests came back from the labs," he told her. "Though in my heart Owen will always be my brother, he is not a Penwyck by blood."

"But how is that possible?" Emily asked. "He's your twin."

Dylan shook his head. "My twin died at birth and was replaced in the nursery with an orphan— Owen—born the night before. Though it sounds cold, my mother did what she needed to do to keep peace and control at the throne and in the palace. Only she knew that my father's brother had attempted to switch me and the child he thought was my twin, but she secretly thwarted his plan and returned Owen and me to the nursery, while the other two babies were sent to the states and adopted. My uncle intended to use this to his advantage at a later date, to take control of Penwyck away from my father by proving that the heirs to the throne were not of his blood."

"Oh, Dylan, how awful." Emily slipped her hand tighter into his. "But Owen—"

"Owen is happy with his new wife and daughter, and he will have an important and valuable position as commander of the Royal Intelligence Institute. He knows that he is loved by all his family, blood or not.''

"And your mother." Emily shook her head sadly. "What a horrible burden she's carried all these years."

Dylan smiled. "My mother has never appeared happier. She says she's ready for a long-overdue extended vacation with my father. I do believe she actually called it a second honeymoon. She also plans on enjoying more grandchildren." He squeezed her hand. "She will be thrilled to learn a third grandchild is on the way."

"Have they forgiven me?" she asked quietly. "Have you forgiven me?"

"There's nothing to forgive." He saw the worry in her eyes, wanted to kiss away every fear. "You did what you did out of love for your grandmother. Once I calmed down, I understood that. And without your cooperation, it might have been years before we apprehended the Black Knights."

"But you were shot." She slipped her hand from his and shook her head. "You could have died. All because of me."

"I fought for my country, for my family's honor," he said firmly. "Now I'm fighting for you, Emily. Please come back to Penwyck with me."

He slid the ring from the box, then slipped it on her finger. Her tears fell onto their joined hands. "I love you," he said, then brushed his lips over hers. "Marry me."

"Here we are. A washcloth." Olivia breezed back

into the room, stopped at the sight of Dylan kneeling before her granddaughter. "Dear me."

Dylan stood, bowed to Olivia. "Mrs. Bridgewater, I ask for your granddaughter's hand in marriage."

"Well, my heavens." Olivia waved the washcloth. "You certainly do work fast, young man."

"Yes, ma'am."

Olivia sized Dylan up, then glanced at Emily. "What do you say, my dear? Do you want to marry this man?"

"Yes, Grandmother. I do."

Olivia lifted her chin and looked down her nose at Dylan. "I certainly can't have my granddaughter marrying riffraff. Can you provide a good living for my Emily?" she demanded.

"Yes, ma'am. I believe I can." He smiled at Olivia, then looked at Emily. She smiled back. "I believe I can."

Three months later, bells rang from the tower of Penwyck Palace. The sound carried across the town, over the mountains, down the cliffs and to the sea. A warm breeze whispered the promise of spring, carried the scent of roses and lilacs and jasmine. Flowers filled every corner of the palace, every stairway, every table. Royal-blue satin covered each chair assembled in the reception hall; white tulle tied with baby-pink roses draped every marble column.

Anticipation shimmered in the early-evening air. Today would make history in Penwyck, for there would be two celebrations: A wedding and a coronation. The event would be televised, and the people of Penwyck crowded around the TVs in their living rooms and in their pubs, waiting for the ceremony to begin.

Twenty trumpets sounded and a hush fell over the reception hall and the island, as well.

"His Majesty, King Morgan Penwyck and Her Majesty, Queen Marissa Penwyck," a page announced.

King Morgan, draped in the royal robe and wearing the jeweled crown, emerged from the back of the hall with Queen Marissa at his side. Her pale-blue beaded gown brought gasps from the women and appreciative glances from the men. Together, king and queen walked down the red carpet toward the waiting throne.

At the front of the hall, Morgan and Marissa's children and their spouses all stood, as did the five hundred other guests in the ballroom.

The trumpets sounded again.

"His Royal Highness, Prince Dylan Edward Penwyck."

A murmur danced over the guests as Dylan appeared in his full formal garb of black pants, gold-buttoned white coat and red sash. He approached his parents, then bowed deeply.

King Morgan stepped forward. "By royal decree, it is my honor and my privilege to pass my crown and the leadership of Penwyck to my son, Prince Dylan Edward Penwyck. I crown thee, His Majesty, King Dylan of Penwyck."

"Long live the king."

The guests cheered and clapped and the trumpets

sounded again. King Morgan bowed to his son, then placed the gold crown on his head and the royal robe on his shoulders.

Once again, the trumpets blared and the crowd quieted. At the sound of the wedding march, all heads turned to the back of the room. Dylan stood straight, kept his gaze on the back entrance.

He watched her emerge in a cloud of white satin and tulle, felt his heart jump into his throat as she floated toward him. The sleeves of the dress were long and snug, and the train extended ten feet. Billows of white tulle covered her face, pearls kissed the base of her throat.

She carried white roses, drifted toward him like a snowflake on a river. He forgot to breathe, could barely think as the vision of the woman he loved glided closer.

It seemed as if everyone in the room held their breath along with their new king. Mouths were agape, eyes filled with tears.

Emily knew that if she kept her own eyes on Dylan, she would not stumble or fall. Her heart swelled with the love she felt for her prince, her king. She moved in front of him, stopped, then curtsied.

He bowed, then offered his hand.

Together they walked up the few steps and stood in front of the priest. Together they said their vows. When he lifted her veil, slipped the ring on her finger, then kissed her, Emily knew that this was forever.

The trumpets blared again. The crowd stood and

cheered, in the hall and across the land. Dylan leaned close for another kiss and she met him halfway.

"I love you, Your Majesty," he said for her ears only.

"And I, you, Your Majesty," she replied.

They turned and bowed, first to Dylan's smiling family and a tearful Olivia Bridgewater, then to their guests and the people of Penwyck.

They walked down the steps together hand-in-hand, as man and wife, as king and queen. Emily nearly stumbled when she felt the first flutter of life inside her. She swallowed back her tears of joy.

Tonight I will tell him, she said silently and pressed a hand to her stomach. She knew he would be pleased.

Not one baby, she thought with a smile, but two.

Twins…

* * * * *

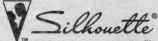

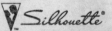